MISMATCHED
SUMMER

MISMATCHED
SUMMER

C.S. ADLER

G. P. PUTNAM'S SONS
New York

Acknowledgment:

With thanks to Dene Williamson and her friend Emily Dachelet, for sharing so frankly with me.

G. P. Putnam's Sons, a division of The Putnam & Grosset Book Group, 200 Madison Avenue, New York, NY 10016. Published simultaneously in Canada.
Printed in the United States of America
Book design by Jean Weiss
Library of Congress Cataloging-in-Publication Data
Adler, C. S. (Carole S.)
Mismatched summer / C.S. Adler.
p. cm. Summary: Two twelve-year-old girls, conscientious Meg and devilish Micale, are forced by their mothers to spend the summer together on Cape Cod and end up expanding each other's horizons.
[1. Friendship—Fiction. 2. Cape Cod (Mass.)—Fiction.]
I. Title. PZ7.A26145Mi   1991 [Fic]—dc20   90-9038 CIP AC
ISBN 0-399-21776-2
10 9 8 7 6 5 4 3 2 1
First Impression

For my darling Ken and Kathy
With hopes for their happy ever-afters

MISMATCHED
SUMMER

You'd think an only child of older parents like me would have some advantages. Like they should think I'm wonderful, not having any other kids to compare me to, and they should give me what I want and let me do what I want. But no way, not in my family. Take this summer. I told them I absolutely would not, repeat, would *not* be dumped on Meg Waters for two months, but there I was on a bus crossing the Cape Cod Canal on my way to guess who. It wasn't that I had anything against Meg. I mean, she can't help that she's totally boring. Boring's probably in her genes like being dynamic's in mine. It was my parents I was mad at. Just because the grandma had broken her hip and wouldn't leave her doctors in Ohio, did *not* mean my mother had to go take care of her. Ma could have made her brother do it. Or she could have hired a nurse and flown out a few times to check up on Grandma. Both those intel-

ligent suggestions were made by me—you betcha—
but Ma shot them down. Zap and out.

"How can you be so selfish, Micale?" Ma had
asked, tromping over my feelings per usual. "This is
the first time your grandma's ever asked me for help,
and I fully intend to give it to her." Ma's big and
queenly. She looked down at me as if I were some
crawly creature she was tempted to squash.

"Listen," I said, "how about if I go with you? You
know how good I am at making people laugh. I
could cheer Grandma up."

"By getting into trouble, you mean?" Ma asked.

"By my natural high spirits and humorousness," I
said, and tried disarming her with a grin.

"It's those natural high spirits that I don't want to
deal with in Ohio. I have to concentrate on Grandma,
not worry about what kind of mischief you're up to,
Micale."

Ma acts like she hates me. About the only time
I catch a warm glint in her eye is when I ace a
report card or remember her birthday. Mostly she
treats me like a hood in one of her eighth-grade
social studies classes. But this time I got in the last
word.

"Ma, in case you haven't noticed, I'm twelve years
old, not two," I said. Then I stalked out of the
kitchen pretending to be tall.

We have one of those big suburban houses where
the kitchen and the living room are equal-sized
arenas. Dad was reading in his leather recliner near

the fireplace in the living room. I circled the Chinese rug that Ma doesn't like anyone in shoes to step on and leaned against the arm of Dad's chair. "How'd you like to have the best taco maker in the family cooking dinner for you this summer, Dadsy?" I asked him.

He blinked at me mildly. It takes him a minute to tune in if anyone disturbs his reading. "I've got to write a research paper for a conference in Hawaii," he said finally.

"Good. Then you'll be glad to have me cook for you while you work. Won't it be a treat, just you and me alone together?"

"I'm planning to eat diet frozen dinners and lose fifteen pounds," he said. "A kitchen full of junk food would dissolve my resolve."

"All right," I promised, "I won't cook anything fattening. You won't *see* a potato chip all summer. No fried anything. I'll even hide my peanut butter."

"Thanks anyway, Micale, but I can't afford distractions. You go stay with your friend and enjoy the beach," he said.

"Meg's not my friend. My friends are here in Saratoga. Meg doesn't even like me. She only likes Ma." Meg had told me once that my mother was her favorite teacher. She stopped me in the hall to say it and left me with my jaw hanging. My mother's the strictest, hardest teacher in our whole middle school. You *know* what kind of kid would like her best.

"Besides, Dad," I said, "Meg's mother probably

only agreed to take me as a favor because Ma stuck up for her."

At that point Dad rattled his paper. "You'd better discuss this with your mother, Micale. I'm reading."

Reading in our house is a sacred activity. Nobody's supposed to bother anybody who's reading. Even when I went through my comic book craze, they'd tiptoe by me if I had one in my hands.

I went back to attack Ma in the kitchen, but she shrugged off my arguments. Finally I shouted, "How can you do this to me?"

And you know what my hard-hearted mother said? She said, "Spending a summer with Meg will be good for you. She's a sensible girl, very mature for her age. And you could do with a little maturing."

I howled. I really howled. Here I am, the personality kid of the century, and do my parents appreciate me? No. They'd rather have a twelve-year-old senior citizen with a frown line like Meg. Well, that's my parents for you. The stork must have delivered me to the wrong chimney.

"Hyannis," the bus driver announced. I saw some people waving, but none of them was Meg or her cute young mother. I climbed onto my seat to pull my tote bag down from the rack, took a deep breath, fixed my smile in place and debussed. I guess if you can deplane, you can debus. Anyway, I got off. Everybody was either waiting for their suitcases or hurrying into the terminal. I had to collect the monster suitcase Mother had packed for me.

I could barely drag it into the terminal, it weighed so much. Ma probably packed it with everything I own hoping to be rid of me for good. Most of what she buys me is pastel—cute little flowery items with ruffles. Even as a baby I didn't look good in that stuff. Jeans and dungaree jackets suit me best.

I couldn't see anyone I knew in the terminal, so I collapsed onto the nearest bench. A guy without any teeth was sitting at the other end mumbling to himself. His head kept jerking up. He was old, but he looked strong enough to be scary. I pulled my railroad cap low over my forehead and slouched down in my seat. When my short hair's tucked under the railroad cap, you can't tell if I'm a girl or a boy. That's good in a place like a bus station where being a girl's dangerous. Considering all the places where it's better to be a boy, I wish I'd been born one.

Not too many people were left in the station now. Everyone who'd gotten off my bus was gone. So where were Meg and her mother? This *was* Hyannis where I was supposed to get off, wasn't it? Maybe Heather Waters wasn't as reliable and responsible as Ma thought. They were just friends during school hours from eating lunch together and yakking in the teachers' room. Or they *used* to yak when Heather was an aide in the principal's office. Maybe those snide remarks people made about Heather being flaky weren't just gossip. Trust Ma to ship her only daughter off to anybody willing to take her, reliable or not.

Another bum headed my way. This one had a bottle sticking out of a paper bag. He kind of leaned into my knees and mumbled something at me. I didn't get what he was saying because my heart was booming in my ears, but I shook my head. He teetered, then moved a few steps and sat down in the middle of the bench. I took a deep breath and held it till my cheeks puffed up.

So if they weren't coming to get me, what should I do? I could find a policeman and say I'd run away from home and changed my mind and would he/she call my folks, please. That would get some action. It wasn't what my buddies Orrin or Louray would do, probably. Probably Orrin would be glad if nobody picked him up. He is always threatening to build himself a shelter in a park and live by scavenging deposit bottles. If my father had hit me with a strap like Orrin's Dad did him, I'd have moved to a park long ago, but Orrin has a little brother he likes. Louray has about ten brothers and sisters, all with different fathers. Of the three of us outsider types, Louray is the most practical. She'd probably sell the clothes out of the suitcase and buy a ticket back home to Saratoga.

Imagine Dad's predicament if I showed up on his doorstep. Since Mom is already on her way to the grandma's and can't tell him what to do, he might just let me stay with him. Or I could buy myself a ticket and go exploring someplace new. That'd be an adventure, except it'd be night when I got there and where does a twelve-year-old kid go at night in a strange city? I couldn't exactly see myself checking into a hotel. What I could imagine was being chased down a dark alley by somebody with a knife, or being bitten by a mad dog or being turned on to drugs and becoming a zombie.

See, under my bold front hides a chicken heart. My mother should only know how hard I have to work at being tough. I could be as boring as Meg if I gave in to myself. Maybe Ma really would like me better that way, but that just shows her bad taste. I wouldn't like me better. I like me gutsy.

I sat up straighter and started thinking brave. Heather Waters was a neat lady, and she liked me. Any minute she'd show up to collect me. Of course, she would. She was one of the few adults in Saratoga who thought I was a cute kid. I calmed down. It's amazing how well you listen to your own advice if nobody else is around.

CHAPTER

TWO

MEG

The gull framed by my bedroom window was just resting on the wind, hanging there in the sky without once flapping its wings. I told myself it was an omen. The gull was Micale, the troublemaker, hovering over my life. "Beat it," I whispered. "Get lost." Suddenly it angled into the wind and took off. But Micale was on her way. In fact, her bus would be in Hyannis before we were if Mom didn't hurry up and get here. Well, it wouldn't scare Micale to be alone for a while in a strange town. Not her. But still it wasn't right for us to be late.

Mom's boss probably had her working too hard to notice the time. What did he care about her problems outside the sandwich shop! She claimed he was good hearted because he had a Santa Claus laugh and told her stories. I wished for the hundredth time that she wasn't so trusting.

Unless she had forgotten. I got off my bed to go

call the sandwich shop, but then I realized they'd never answer during the noontime rush. Besides, Mom wouldn't forget. I was just being nervous.

I looked over my shoulder at the bed by the door that I'd made up for Micale. What could I say if she wanted the window side of the room? I'd already shoved my clothes to the window side of the closet and dresser. Now, to make sure she got the picture, I took the Barbie doll in basketball uniform that my team had given me when we beat Clifton Park, and propped it against my pillow. The room was so small and musty and dark. Micale would want the window all right. But I needed it. I needed to see the pink and gold sunrise and the stars that seemed brighter here and bigger than in Saratoga. Sometimes, looking out the window, I almost flowed into the sky. Then I'd feel peaceful as that gull riding the wind.

The horn honked. Mom! I ran out the kitchen door and climbed into Aunt Jane's rusty pickup. We were driving it because Mom had to give up her car when she couldn't afford the finance charges anymore. "You all right?" I asked her.

"Fine. I'm sorry I'm late. George and I were going like a pair of windmills trying to keep up with the orders. Isn't it wonderful he's so busy when the season hasn't even started yet?"

"Yeah, wonderful for George. Is he going to hire anyone to help you?"

"He's trying, Meg."

Mom claimed she'd been lucky to land the sandwich shop job the minute we got to Wellfleet back in May. She'd been told jobs were hard to find on the Cape before the tourist season started. Maybe, but she'd had it a lot easier as an aide in my school's office in Saratoga. Besides, I used to wait for her after the last bell, and we'd exchange the news of the day as she drove us home. Then we'd make dinner together. Here, I spend a lot of time alone and mostly make the dinner by myself. Then soon after we eat, Mom'll start yawning and head off to bed. She loves the beach as much as I do, but she hasn't had a chance to enjoy it yet.

"Aren't you a little excited that Micale's coming?" Mom asked me.

"More like a little worried," I said.

Mom gave me her perky smile. "It'll be fine. She'll be company, and at least she's someone you know."

"Ummm," I said. Why make Mom feel bad by pointing out that I don't want to be around anyone I know? After the newspaper story came out about what Mom almost did to her boyfriend, people in Saratoga stared at us as if we were freaks. Even some friends acted weird. I'll never forget how Sue Ellen Potts ducked past me in the halls and never gave me an invitation to her big Easter party. Even if it was her mother's fault, the way my other friends said, Sue Ellen knows my mother's a good person. She should have stuck up for Mom.

A cardinal flew across the road from the locust grove. "Look," Mom said.

"Beautiful," I mumbled, still thinking about Saratoga and the newspaper article. The reporter never mentioned that just because Mom wouldn't give her boyfriend our mortgage payment he broke two of her ribs and punched her in the face. If Mom hadn't picked up the kitchen knife and threatened him with it, he might have killed her. And why did the police take so long to get there? I called them the minute I walked into the kitchen and saw Mom in trouble. They should have come right away and arrested him before Mom grabbed the knife. "Woman Threatens Boyfriend with Knife," the headline had said. What kind of news reporting was that when they didn't say why?

"Where did your mother pick up a man like that?" the woman I baby-sat for had asked me.

"In the supermarket," I'd said. "He wanted advice on potatoes."

She meant to be sympathetic, but questions like that made me sick. I'd thought the guy was nice, too, when I first met him, so friendly and sort of cute-looking. He'd said he was temporarily unemployed. Maybe it was the six months of job hunting without getting an offer that turned him into a maniac. But anyway, he gave us an awful experience. My stomach didn't stop aching until we got to Cape Cod and became anonymous.

Mom stopped at the corner of Cove Road and waited for a hole to open up in the Route 6 traffic. "You're very quiet, Meg," she said. "You aren't mad at me for saying yes to Edna Elder, are you?"

"It was just as much my fault as yours," I said.

That was the truth. I'd been in the kitchen with Mom when Mrs. Elder called. Mom covered the receiver with her hand so Micale's mother couldn't hear, and said, "Edna's mother broke her hip and she's off to Ohio to take care of her. How would you feel about Micale spending the summer in Wellfleet with us?"

Terrible, I should have said immediately. Instead I thought about how Mrs. Elder had stuck up for Mom with the School Board. They wanted to get rid of her after the newspaper made her sound like the guilty party. We had a copy of the letter Mrs. Elder sent saying what a fine person Mom was, and hard working and helpful and upstanding, and how everybody liked her. Even though they eliminated Mom's job in the budget cuts anyway—a sneaky way of firing her—I was still grateful to Mrs. Elder for trying. She's been a real friend to Mom, and she's been good to me, too. She stayed after school and helped me make up the work I'd missed while I was home taking care of Mom. Not to mention that she's the only teacher I've had who ever made social studies interesting. She even suggested I think about a foreign service career since I'm so good at languages. She said I was a "natural diplomat" and that people turned to me for advice and expected me to smooth things over. Getting a compliment like that from Mrs. Elder really pleased me. Only she doesn't know what a bad temper I have. Well, I control it. Anyway, Mom and I owed Mrs. Elder too much to say no to her.

What I had done was stall. "Wouldn't Micale be better off going to camp or someplace?" I'd asked my mother, who still had her hand over the phone.

Mom shook her head. "Mrs. Elder says Micale hates organized activities. We could do it, Meg, if you'd share your room."

"Yeah, but—" I squirmed and said, "Mom, I don't like Micale and I'm sure she doesn't like me either."

"What do you mean? Remember what I told you she said about you when she was waiting to see the principal? You know, after she started the food fight in the cafeteria? She said how much she admires your strength of character."

What could I say after that except, "Well, if she wants to come . . ."

That was all Mom needed to hear. She promptly told Mrs. Elder we'd love to have Micale.

Next thing I knew, Mom was saying things into the phone like, "That's not necessary," and, "But we're friends, Edna. You wouldn't let me pay *you* if you were taking Meg for the summer." Finally she said, "Well, all right, if you put it that way . . ."

Mom hung up and turned to me. I asked, "Mrs. Elder's going to pay us to take care of Micale?"

"She really wants to, Meg."

"But you shouldn't let her. It's embarrassing."

Mom looked hurt. Quietly she said, "Edna knows

how strapped we are this summer, Meg, and she can afford to pay us. She said we're doing her a tremendous favor, that Micale's a handful and she wouldn't know who else to leave her with . . . Sometimes you have to sit on your pride and accept help, darling."

I shut up. I'd watched Mom deciding which bills to pay and which to put off another month even before she lost her job. And now she was considering selling our house in Saratoga to pay off our debts. I'd grown up in that house and I loved it, but so what. I didn't want to go back to Saratoga, even though I was supposed to be class secretary this fall besides being captain of the girls' basketball team. Still, taking money from Mrs. Elder instead of returning the favor we owed her made me squirm.

We passed Blackfish Creek, which is a huge marshy cove that stretches clear out to the bay. Mom asked, "You don't really *hate* Micale, do you?"

I considered before answering that. "I hated her when we were in the same class in third grade. She was always talking out of turn and making us lose our points for being good, and we never got a free period on Fridays. Everybody hated her for that, her and her big mouth . . . And I don't think she's improved."

"You don't think she's funny?"

"She's a show-off." I thought of last year when Mrs. Elder invited Mom and me for tea and Micale greeted us at the door in Mrs. Elder's beaded blouse, which was dress length on Micale. She said her mother had told her to dress like a lady for a change. After Mrs. Elder made her change, Micale asked if I wanted to see the house. I did because I like Mrs. Elder and I'd never been in her house before. It's big and in a fancy development, but Micale didn't need to mock it like she did. She introduced her parents' bedroom as "the royal chambers" and the bathroom with the Jacuzzi as "the throne room." "Ma likes things rich," Micale said in a kind of sneering way.

I thought the house was beautiful, especially the kitchen. The wall tiles had raised pictures of plants done by an artist. A row of copper pans hung from wood beams that crossed the high ceiling, and everything in the place shone.

"Anyway, Micale *must* like you," Mom said without taking her eyes off the road ahead.

"How do you figure that?"

"Why would she want to spend the summer with you?"

"It wasn't her idea, was it?"

"No, but she could have gone to camp."

"Mom, believe me. The only kids Micale likes are the ones she knows from the bench in the principal's office. I don't know why she's coming here, but I bet her mother's making her. Mrs. Elder's your friend and I think she likes me."

"Well," Mom said, "she did say that she expects you to be a good influence on Micale."

"She did? Oh no! Just what I need. If she told Micale that, we'll end up killing each other."

Mom laughed. She took one hand from the wheel long enough to pinch my cheek affectionately.

"I can't see what you like about Micale," I grumbled.

"Well, she's lively. And I feel sort of sorry for her."

"Sorry for her?"

"Sure. She's a late-in-life child, and she and her mother don't have a good relationship . . . I guess I feel lucky that you and I are so close. Have I ever told you that you're the prize in my Cracker Jack box, Meg?"

I smiled. She had, lots of times.

"And I think Micale's funny. She makes me laugh," Mom continued.

"Funny! I didn't know you liked practical jokes. That's her kind of funny. Personally I think practical jokes are stupid."

Mom giggled. "But that picture she did on the school door of the principal as Dracula *was* clever."

"Sure it was. You think mocking people's great, Mom?"

"No, but basically Micale's a good kid," Mom said. "And she doesn't deserve the way Edna puts her down all the time. Edna's a smart woman. She ought to know better than to go around calling Micale 'my demon daughter.'"

"So how would you feel if you were a teacher and the principal kept calling you down to the office about your own daughter? Like when Micale turned a stall in the girls' room into a shrine with flowers and a plaster saint? Personally *I* feel sorry for Mrs. Elder."

"Well," Mom said cheerfully, "it'll be good for them both to get away from each other for a few months. And I bet Micale will behave herself with us . . . Anyway, you've always been able to get along with people, honey. Remember, she'll be our guest. Okay?" That was as close to laying down the law to me as my mother gets.

I heaved a rib-lifting sigh, and she changed the subject.

"Did you get to the clam beds this morning?"

"Sure," I said.

"Maybe Micale will help you with that job. I feel guilty sticking you with it so often."

"Why? I like outdoor work. You know that."

"Still," Mom said. "I'm probably violating the child labor laws letting you take care of those seed clams."

Our deal with Aunt Jane was that we got the cottage free for the summer in exchange for checking her clam beds. Aunt Jane had been waiting forever for this grant to a part of the bay, and no sooner did she get it and seed the beds with baby clams than she had to go take care of her inheritance in Missouri. This way, we could stay in her cottage, rent out *our* house in Saratoga, and come out ahead moneywise.

Mom was craning her neck at the traffic coming around the rotary at Orleans. We still had a good way to go on Route 6 before we turned off to Hyannis and the bus station. "You know," she said, "it wouldn't hurt if Micale influenced you a little, too. I'd like to see you act silly once in a while."

I felt as if she'd hit me. "Silly? You want me to be silly?"

"It's just I worry that you're missing something."

"Well, I'm not," I assured her.

"I put too much responsibility on your shoulders."

"I like responsibility."

We'd been over this ground before. She was always worrying that she wasn't a good-enough mother. To head her off, I said flat out, "Mom, I couldn't ask for a better mother."

Mom shook her head. She went into the bit about how scared she'd been when my father walked out on her and she was only nineteen and had me to take care of. Then she told her other favorite single-motherhood story, that once she'd taken me along on a date because she couldn't get a sitter and I'd slept right through the whole evening, angelic me. I've gotten old enough to wonder what her date must have thought about having a baby along. I bet *he* never took Mom out again.

"You were always such a reasonable child, Meg, so good." Mom got tears in her eyes. She usually did when she talked about my childhood. But she couldn't possibly see the road very well with tears in her eyes.

I gave her a quick kiss to reassure her. "Mom, we're doing fine."

"You bet," she said, and signed off as always with,

"You know, the one thing I'm grateful to your father for was that he gave me you."

Finally she started chatting away about the funny people who came into the sandwich shop. I was glad to hear her sounding relaxed, but instead of listening, I was remembering the time in third grade when the teacher made Micale and me partners to write a puppet show. Micale insisted that she was going to write it and I should make the puppets. I did my part, and the night before the project was due I also wrote the show, because Micale was still talking and not working. Micale said what I wrote was boring, and she scribbled a few pages in homeroom, and the teacher let her do it. The show was so bad that I felt like a fool. Being anywhere near Micale has always been a disaster for me.

I recognized her by the railroad cap and the slump. Micale was practically lying on her shoulders. When Mom called her name, she looked up with a big smile and yelled out, "What took you so long?" As I expected, she didn't sound scared, but she gave us a hard time for making her wait. I let Mom apologize while I lugged Micale's giant suitcase out to the pickup. I reached the truck just before my arms pulled out of their sockets. Mom followed with Micale's tote bag. Micale sidestepped along empty-handed, excitedly telling us all the things she'd planned to do if we didn't show up. I could just see her marching into a police station to inform them that she'd changed her mind and didn't want to run away after all.

"You're smiling, Meg," Micale said. "Does that mean you're glad to see me?"

"So far," I said. Then I climbed into the pickup hoping for the best.

CHAPTER

THREE

MICALE

"We're off!" I shouted as Heather turned the ignition key. Meg was scrunched in between her mother and me, which didn't stop her from giving me a sidewise "Down, girl" look. I grinned back at her.

"How's your grandmother doing?" Heather asked me. Heather doesn't even know my grandmother, but that's the kind of question adults think they should ask.

"Good," I said. "She's so glad to get my mother to herself for the summer that she's even stopped griping."

"A broken hip's a serious thing in an older woman," Heather Waters said.

"I guess, but the grandma's a tough old bird. Even Ma expects her to be hitting the shopping malls again in no time, and Ma's no optimist."

While Heather and I did the chitchatting, Meg was just sitting there staring out the window. Don't ask

me at what. The highway was lined with a bunch of
stumpy, green trees and nothing much else. Finally
we went around a rotary and I spotted an ice cream
stand and said, "Yay, civilization at last!"

Meg looked at me as if I were nuts. "Don't you
like ice cream?" I asked her innocently. I've always
enjoyed shaking her up. She's not a phony like most
of the kids in Saratoga, but she's uptight, stuffed
with notions about what's proper.

"Sure I like ice cream," Meg said.

Before I could work up a hot discussion of favorite
brands and flavors, Heather pointed out a salt pond
and a building that she said was the National Seashore Headquarters. "Uh-huh," I said. The salt pond
didn't look special, just round and wet, but next we
passed a miniature-golf course. "Hey, miniature golf.
That's my best sport," I said. "Do you like it, Meg?"

"It's okay," Meg said.

"What Meg likes best is the beach," Heather Waters said. "She's a beach nut."

"Me, too," I said. "I go mad at the smell of salt air
mixed with French fries and popcorn and taffy. I
can't even resist cotton candy, which makes me
throw up."

"The beaches in Wellfleet are pretty quiet,"
Heather Waters warned.

"No boardwalk? No arcades? No rides?"

"No nothing but sand and water," Meg said like
she was boasting.

"So then what do you do for fun?" I asked her.
"Build sand castles?"

"Just hang out," Meg said. "And swim. And sometimes I check out my aunt's clam beds."

"Yes, Meg gets stuck with that job," her mother said, "because you can only do it at low tide, which always seems to come when I'm at work."

From what I knew of Meg, I figured she probably didn't mind. She is the kind of kid who always volunteers for boring jobs like note taking or book counting or ticket selling. Looking at her profile next to her mother's was funny. Her mother's face was open and sunny. Meg's was so crammed with thoughts and so serious that she looked older than her mother. That can't be healthy for a twelve-year-old kid.

"You know," I said to Meg's mom, "it's hard to think of you as Mrs. Waters when you look so good in jeans. Could I call you Heather?"

"Oh? Well, why not?" She laughed as if the compliment tickled her.

Meg raised an eyebrow, but didn't say anything. She makes you guess what she's thinking, but her face is pretty easy to read.

"Do you like steamers?" Heather wanted to know.

"What are they?"

"Clams. Meg and I love them. We eat them once a week."

"Well," I said uneasily, "I'm sort of allergic to clams."

"Sort of allergic?"

"I break out in hives. Big ones. Mostly I stay clear of seafood. Anything *fried* I can eat."

Mother and daughter exchanged a heavy-duty look. "Listen," I reassured them. "I'm no problem to feed. I can live on peanut butter sandwiches."

"For breakfast, lunch and dinner?" Meg asked.

"And snacks, too," I promised.

We turned left at a supermarket that was the only store I'd seen since we passed the movie theater miles back. "Meg walks to this market to pick up any extras we need," Heather said. "It's about a mile and a half from the cottage. And the post office is here too. Kind of convenient."

I nodded agreeably and didn't mention that I only walk when I have to. And my mother claims I say everything I think without thinking!

We drove down a woodsy road. Again there was water to my right, beginning with a marshy-looking edge. "That's the town of Wellfleet across the cove," Heather said. I saw a marina and some buildings so far away they were toy sized—a lot of trees, a few houses and no people. If that was the nearest town, the hike to the market might be the big thrill of my days. I didn't say that out loud either.

We went up a hill and down sandy lanes lined with cottages. Finally Heather chirruped, "Here you are. Aunt Jane's cottage. Home-sweet-home until the end of August." We were in the middle of a jumble of tacky-looking cottages surrounded by sand. The shack we parked behind was covered with gray shingles that looked ready to blow off in the next big wind, except the cottage had obviously been there since the Pilgrims landed. I saw a beat-up picnic table next to a rusty barbecue grill and a clothesline.

As we unloaded my things from the truck, Heather said, "Wish I could stay and go for a swim with you girls, but I'm due back at work. So glad you're here, Micale." She hugged me warmly and added, "Anything you need, just ask. We want you to have a fun summer." She beamed at me, but before I'd soaked up her welcome, she said, "See you later," and left.

Meg was struggling toward the cottage with my suitcase. She looked back at me. I gave her a big smile. She didn't give me anything. Oh boy, loosening her up was going to be a tough job. I took a deep breath to rev myself up and said, "Great air. You can smell the fish and seaweed."

She squinted at me doubtfully and asked, "You want to bring in your other bag, Micale?"

"Sure thing," I said cheerfully. I lugged my tote after her through the back door into the kitchen. It was so small I felt like apologizing to the refrigerator for crowding it.

"We spend most of our time in the living room," Meg said as she bumped the suitcase through another doorway. She gave her aunt's living room a critical once-over. It looked pretty shabby with its beat-up maple furniture and rag rug, but shabby's my style. Apparently the living room did double duty as a dining room because there by the window was a table with a paper-napkin holder and salt and pepper shakers on it.

I sprawled on the threadbare brown plaid sofa and said, "Hey, I like this place."

"You like it?" Meg sounded disbelieving.

"Sure. At home, I have to tiptoe around trying not to sweat on the upholstery. Here, not to worry, right?" I spotted a bookcase in the hallway. "Anything good to read?"

"Well, there's lots to choose from. Aunt Jane buys trunkloads of books at the library sale every year."

"Mysteries?"

"Everything. When the weather's bad, all you can do is read . . . There's a few old games. You know, Scrabble and Monopoly."

"Sounds fun," I said. "I like board games. Do you like Stephen King? I can lend you his latest, soon as I finish it."

"No thanks. Mostly I read biographies or romance."

"Do you have a boyfriend?" I asked.

"A boyfriend? No. Do you?"

"Nope. See, we do have *something* in common."

That brought a half smile. Chalk up one point for me.

Next Meg showed me this dark hole of a bedroom and said the side near the door was mine. I caught guilt in her tone. Well, it was fine with me if she wanted the window side. I like being able to roll out of bed and get to the bathroom easily in the middle of the night. But I jiggled the hook a little to test her.

"Sometimes I have trouble breathing at night," I

said. "Used to have asthma. Maybe I should be nearer the window."

"Oh," Meg said. Glum face. Intake of breath. "Well, okay, then I guess we'd better switch sides."

Now what fun is it if she gives in so easy? "How about we switch off, and one week I get the window and the next it's yours?" I suggested.

"No." Still glum. "I don't like moving around."

"So you don't care about the window that much?" I probed.

She cared all right. Enough to get tears in her eyes. "Well," she said, "I like watching the stars, and birds and—"

"Tell you what," I said. "We'll flip for it."

She nodded. That gave her a chance at least. I won the first flip, so I suggested two out of three. "That's fairer," I said to impress her with what a good person I really am. Finally she won. "Okay, it's yours," I said.

"But what about your breathing?"

"Just don't use up all the air before it gets to me," I said.

That made her laugh.

I shoved my humongous suitcase over to the head of the bed and stood it on end. "Presto—a night table."

"Don't you want to unpack it first?"

"What for? Everything I need's in my tote."

She eyed the tote. "We could go for a swim after lunch if you've got a suit in there."

"I already had my lunch on the bus. Ma made me two peanut butter sandwiches, the way I like them without the crusts . . . Is there a pool?"

"A *pool*? What for? We have a whole bay to swim in."

"A bay, huh? Well, you go ahead and I'll watch you. I'm strictly a pool person." Ever since I got beaten up by the waves on a seashore vacation, I haven't trusted water unless it's been walled up. Let me tell you, it's no fun being rolled on rocks and choked with gallons of salt water.

"But if you don't swim," Meg said, "what'll you do for fun here?"

"I'll figure out something." She looked so worried I asked, "Will I make the *Guinness Book of World Records* if I never swim in the bay this summer?"

"Probably," she said, still frowning.

I couldn't wait to spring my first gift on her and watch her reaction. If she had a kid caged up in her somewhere, I was going to find it.

She got into a pink and white striped swimsuit that my mother would have loved. Ma thinks girls and pink are synonymous. Actually, Meg looked good in that suit. She's built and she's got long legs. Me, I'm short and bowlegged and my rear end sticks out too much, which of course means Ma had to pick a suit with a bow like a bustle in the back for me. "It's blue. I thought you like blue," Ma complained when I wouldn't try it on. No doubt it was somewhere in the big suitcase with all the rest of the Barbie doll clothes she'd selected.

To get to the beach, we walked over a dune on a narrow path between two cottages. I grabbed a fistful of the two-foot-high grass blades and it bit back. "Ow, what is this stuff?" I complained.

"Dune grass," Meg said. "It has to be tough to grow in the sand."

"It's tough enough to use in a knife fight," I said.

The beach was a flat tan belt of sand, and the water was calm, but it went on forever out to the horizon. That was scary for a one-lap swimmer like me. Houses perched on the low dunes behind the beach like a funny row of birds, and to our left was like a river that Meg said was dry at low tide. Some fishing boats far out on the bay were the only signs of life, except for a few finger-sized people way down the beach. I was used to populated beaches where somebody might notice if you were drowning.

"It's really quiet here," I said.

"Yes." Suddenly Meg was sounding enthusiastic. "And it's always different no matter when you come."

"You mean once in a while there's other people?"

"I mean there's low tide when the sandpipers and gulls are out looking for food. And at high tide, the water might be pounding the wall there. And the wind's always changing the water and the sky around . . . The sun goes down that way." She pointed to the right.

"Uh-huh." I was amazed that anyone could like a place that didn't even have a Coke machine.

"Well, I'm going to swim," Meg said. "Want to change your mind?"

"Nope." I pulled off my sneakers and did a cartwheel in the sand to prove I wasn't a total couch potato. Meg didn't seem impressed. She splashed into the water, dove under and came up swimming hard parallel to shore. Not a lifeguard in sight either. Imagine having a mother so young she didn't worry about drowning! My mother'd have a fit if she saw me swim without a lifeguard handy.

I ambled over some brown strawy stuff to test the water temperature. My toes curled in protest at the cold. Still, I was considering wading as a possibility when a crab the size of my hand scuttled by. I jerked my foot out of the water and backed away. Crabs! I hate crabs. Meg was still swimming. The crabs hadn't gotten to her yet. I watched her plowing the water. The furrows kept disappearing as fast as she made them.

Oh boy, I thought, I should have gone to camp. They couldn't make me participate in physical activities there either, but at least I'd have kids to fool around with. Here there was only Meg, and what if she had no kid in her to find? Two things I remembered about her from third grade. The first was how furious she'd been with me for not writing the puppet play we were supposed to do. I wanted to, but I just couldn't think of anything and I didn't want her to think I was lazy, so I came up with some dumb thing at the last minute. It must have been really bad because the teacher barely gave us a passing grade. I should have let Meg use her play, but it was so boring—all about a kid buying a birthday present for his mother.

The other thing I remembered was the time when my classmates threw mud balls at me on the playground because I'd made them lose their free period again. Meg had been the one who stopped them. She told them if they didn't leave me alone, she'd tell the teacher and they'd really be in trouble. I asked her afterward why she'd stuck up for me. "Because there were six of them and only one of you," she'd said. But there'd been only one of her, too. In her own way, Meg's as brave as my friends Orrin and Louray. I've always admired people who are brave. I'd just have to keep trying things with Meg and see what I could make of her. After all, even apes are born knowing how to play.

FOUR

MEG

I don't think when I swim. I just swim, but it's like the water massages me inside and out. So when I came out, I was feeling good.

All that stuff Micale had said about liking honky-tonk beaches and eating only peanut butter made me think she was going to be even more of a pain than I'd expected, but not recognizing great swimming when she saw it didn't make her a bad person. And she was our guest. Mom had brought me up to believe guests should get the best of everything you had. Until Micale did something really obnoxious, I'd try to be nice to her.

She was still standing there in the hot sun in her jeans and jacket and railroad cap, but now she was talking to the lady who swims with her big brown poodle. Micale tossed a ball, and the dog sprang straight up after it just like a kangaroo.

"Can you believe the way this goofy beast jumps?" Micale asked me.

The lady's happy smile stayed put even though her dog had been insulted. Her smile and her freckles had made me want to talk to her before, but I'm no good at starting conversations with strangers, and when I tried petting her dog once, it hid behind her and wouldn't let me touch it. Usually animals like me. Not this one. It liked Micale.

"Billie's an Irish water spaniel," Micale said. "I thought he was a poodle."

"She," the lady said. "Billie's a girl, named after a singer, Billie Holiday. I name all my dogs after singers."

"Really?" Micale sounded fascinated. "How many dogs do you have?"

"Right now just Billie, but I used to have Ella Fitzgerald, and before that was Sophie Tucker." Billie nudged Micale who petted the dog's brown curls absentmindedly. I felt a smidge jealous.

"Micale tells me she's visiting you for the summer," the lady said to me. "Aren't you lucky!"

No way I could respond honestly to that. I just smiled back at her.

Later, when I was in the kitchen starting supper and Micale was there watching me, she said, "Mrs. Ryan's nice, but that's one weird dog with its little rat tail and the way it's scared of people."

"Not of you, though."

"No, not of me. Animals like me. People do, too, until they find out I'm freaky."

"So why be freaky?"

"Because that's who I am. I'm not going to change to please anybody. You wouldn't either, would you?"

I looked at her. "It depends," I said. In some ways I wouldn't change, like even if my friends smoked or drank and wanted me to, I wouldn't. On the other hand, I work at keeping a lid on my temper because I care what people think of me.

"I watched you swimming," Micale said. "You're really good, Meg. Ever think of joining a swim team?"

"If we move someplace that has one, I might."

"You're not going back to Saratoga? But what about your house?"

"We'll probably sell it. Mom lost her job there, remember?"

"But she could find another one," Micale said. "You don't want to move, do you?"

"Sometimes I do. After what happened, sometimes I think we'd be better off in a new place."

I crouched down to get the pans I needed out of the cabinet. When I looked up, Micale was frowning. She said, "What do you mean, 'what happened'? Oh, that stuff about your mother's boyfriend? He ought to go to jail. That's what my mother said."

"Well, but some people—lots of people—think it was Mom's fault. You should have seen the anonymous notes we got after they printed that article."

"Nobody who knew your mom could blame her. She's a real sweetie pie. Every time I landed in the office, she'd act like it must be a mistake, me being such a good kid . . . Besides, she laughs at my jokes."

That explained why Micale had come to us this summer. She liked Mom. Well, that was another thing we had in common.

"How come you're making the dinner?" Micale wanted to know. "You don't do it every day, do you?"

"Not every day, and not if we're eating fish. Mom does fish because I always overcook it."

"I've never cooked much," Micale said. "Once I tried to make cookies and almost burned the house down. Ma gets nervous when I go near her kitchen."

"Don't you do the dishes?"

"Listen, you know my mother. Everything's got to be her way. I don't stack the dishwasher right. I don't even make my bed to suit her. Setting the table's all she'll trust me to do, and then she crabs that I don't help around the house. Ma gets her kicks complaining about me."

I was tempted to tell Micale how uncomfortable it made me to hear her criticize her mother, but I didn't. She'd already said she wasn't going to change herself to please anybody. "If you want, you can help make dinner here," I said.

"No thanks. I'll just watch." Micale hitched the chair around and straddled it. She began chatting away about dogs and how she loved them, but her mother wouldn't let her keep any hairy pet that might make dirt in the house. "Ma's death on dirt.

Besides, she considers me animal enough," Micale said.

"Why do you talk as if you don't like her?" I blurted out.

"Because I don't."

"You don't like your own mother?"

"Shocked you, huh? Well, Ma's not wild about me either. She'd trade me in for you in a minute. Do you always like your mother?"

"Yes," I said. "We're good friends."

"Well, Heather's young . . . and that makes a difference," Micale said. "You can do things together, right?"

"We used to. We'd go to movies or take walks or just hang out. But lately, she's been too busy. But there's still little things."

"Like what?"

"Oh, little things . . . Like I'll sit on the floor at her knees while we watch T.V. and she'll brush my hair."

"And you *like* that?" Micale asked. "When I was little and my mother brushed my hair, I screamed bloody murder. That's why I keep it short, so it doesn't need brushing . . . Can I have a spoon?"

As she talked, Micale had been making a musical scale with glasses of water. I gave her a spoon and she started ringing notes. "You could set the table, if you want something to do," I suggested.

"Mmmm," she said, still concentrating on the glasses.

"Jingle Bells," that's what she was playing, I real-

ized. Next thing I knew she'd disappeared. I was at
the refrigerator getting out the tomatoes to finish off
the salad. Relax, I told myself. It's only her first day.
She doesn't need to pitch in and help you out yet. I
set the table in the living room and took the hamburgers off the stove. They were cooked on one side
and would be ready a couple of minutes after Mom
got home. I started cutting up a zucchini to steam.

"I don't think I want any salad," a voice said
shakily.

I turned and saw Micale staring at the bowl that
I'd set on the table. An enormous black spider was
sitting on my lovely greens. I screeched and grabbed
a fly swatter to flip it off. Some of the greens flipped
off with it. Plastic!

"Very funny," I said through clenched teeth.

"It's realistic, isn't it?" Micale looked proud of
herself. "I've got a whole set of bugs at home, but
the spider's the best. I bought it for you."

"Gee, thanks," I said.

"It's a joke," Micale explained, as if maybe I
hadn't understood that.

"I hate practical jokes," I burst out. Then I bit my
lip, ashamed of losing my temper over something so
silly.

Mom came in just as I finished wiping up the
floor. "Hi, love. Smells good in here." She gave me a
big hug and a kiss. Then she hugged Micale. "I'm
bushed," Mom said as she kicked off her shoes.
"And tonight I'm going to something called a dips-

and-spreads workshop with my boss." She sprawled in the chair, yawning and wriggling her toes.

"He said you have to go?" I asked.

"No, sweetie. It sounded interesting so I asked if I could."

"Why do you want to learn about dips and spreads?" I asked. "Are you going to make a career out of sandwiches?"

"Who knows? Maybe I'll become a caterer," Mom said. "George did catering in Chicago before his divorce."

"I thought he used to run a ferry boat. And didn't he tell you he was a fisherman in Alaska?"

"Well, he's an interesting man, Meg. What's wrong with that?"

"Nothing. I just don't understand why you'd spend your free time with him after working with him all day."

"Meg, I thought you'd be pleased that I'm going out. And you have Micale. You two can do something fun together."

"Fun, did I hear the word *fun*?" Micale asked from the doorway. "What's there to do here in the evening?"

"Walk to the breakwater and see the sunset," I said absently. George had an earring in one ear and a gut that strains his shirt buttons. Mom couldn't be considering him romantically, could she?

I heard Mom laughing and tuned in. "What?" I asked.

"I said all this nature stuff was taking my breath away," Micale answered me. "A mall, a mall. I need a mall." She staggered around, holding her throat as if she were choking.

I didn't see what was so funny. Shut up and serve the hamburgers, I told myself. So I did.

We'd just finished the dishes when a delivery truck with the words GEORGE'S GOURMET SAND-WICHES painted on the side pulled up. Mom hurried off to the bathroom and sent me out to greet George. The earring went with a gray beard and a headful of gray curls. His grin went ear to ear. He didn't even say hello before he started off teasing me. "So, here's Meg, the perfect daughter. You know, I offered your mother a shrimp salad sandwich to name your faults, but she said you didn't have any."

I couldn't help smiling because it was nice that Mom boasted about me. "I have lots of faults," I said.

"Your mother doesn't think so. Tell you what. Name me one of your mother's faults and *you* get the shrimp salad."

"Shrimp's her favorite, not mine."

He laughed. "You women! . . . Cookies then, can I bribe you with cookies?"

"Mother's only fault is that she doesn't see the bad things in people until it's too late," I said.

He stopped smiling and drew back to study me. "Then you must feel a need to protect her," he said.

"I try—when she lets me."

Micale had been talking to her mother on the phone. Now she came out to the patio, and seeing the sign on the truck, she said to George, "Hi, I'm Micale. What's gourmet about your sandwiches?"

"The freshest bakery breads and high-quality ingredients. Only the best lettuce leaves and sun-ripened tomatoes." He made a kissing gesture with his fingers.

"Did you ever try peanut butter and bacon and chili?" she asked.

He beamed at her. "You've just created next week's secret sandwich."

"Really? Do I get a commission?" Micale asked.

"Only if it sells. I must tell you I don't get too many orders for secret sandwiches. With their stomachs, people don't take risks."

"How come you wear an earring?" Micale had the nerve to ask him.

"Because I wanted to grow up to be a pirate, but I had too much respect for the law. An earring is the best I could do."

Mom came out in a skirt and blouse. She'd even put on eye makeup. "See you girls later," she said. "Enjoy the sunset."

As soon as she and George were gone, I panicked. She hadn't been out with a man since the guy who'd beaten her up. Oh, I'd liked some of the men she'd dated, but new ones always made me nervous. They'd turn out to be drinkers or want to move in with us right away or just not be willing to commit themselves; and the way my mom was, it didn't take her long to decide she was in love and this was the guy she wanted to spend the rest of her life with. Then when they broke up, she'd be in a bad way. It seemed to me she gave too much too fast and got too little in return. Of course, this was her first date with George. First dates are usually safe. Except George didn't look that old or tame to me. I wanted to run after the truck and make them take me with them, but I knew that was crazy.

"Ow, these mosquitoes are killing me," Micale said. She was slapping her arms. I went to get the bug juice and we sprayed each other's bare skin. Mom was on her own now. I couldn't do anything, just hope George behaved himself. My heart slowed to normal speed. Micale and I set off for the break-water.

It was dead low tide. Way out in the bay, the water was like a huge mirror reflecting the pink and yellow of the sunset, but Micale just nodded when I said how beautiful it was.

"That George is some character," she said. "I liked him. Didn't you?"

"I don't know."

"Your mother sure seems to like him."

"That's what worries me."

"Meg," Micale said, "don't you ever relax and re-member you're a kid?"

"Ummm," I said. "Okay. We can play a game when we get back."

"Hey, you don't have to entertain me. I can watch T.V. or read. It's not me I'm thinking about. It's you."

My eyes filled up with tears. I felt helpless and miserable all of a sudden. "You didn't have to come, Micale," I said. "You should have picked a more fun place to go to."

"Listen," she said. "I make my own fun."

I wiped my eyes with the back of my hand and mumbled, "I just don't think we like the same things."

"Right," Micale said cheerfully. "So one of us has to change."

Not me, I thought, but all I said was, "We're going to miss the sunset if we don't hurry."

Sunsets make me feel dreamy. I stared out toward the darkening cliffs of Chequesset Neck. Wispy clouds were spilling pink into the gold above them. It was a lovely, sad, still evening. Even the gulls were standing in a quiet clump, not screeching at each other. People were dark silhouettes in twos and threes by the rocks as we passed the public beach. A man was snapping pictures of the sunset with a camera on a tripod. Seeing other people enjoy the sunset gives me a good feeling, like I'm sharing something.

"How far are we going?" Micale wanted to know.

"We don't have to go all the way to the breakwater," I said because she sounded tired. "I mean, if you don't want to."

"No, that's okay." Micale kept walking. She

kicked some oyster shells aside and asked me what a horseshoe crab was. When I explained that it'd been around since dinosaur times without changing much, she wanted to know if horseshoe crabs could bite.

"Not unless you back into the tail," I said. I was being funny, but she gave me a questioning look. She'd be pretty if she dressed like a girl. Her face is kind of heart shaped, and she has bright brown eyes and a little nose. I'd never noticed how pretty she was.

"I should have brought my boom box," Micale said.

"People around here don't like boom boxes," I warned. "They call the police on you if you make a lot of noise."

"I was thinking of making music, not noise," Micale said. "You know, to liven the place up." She wriggled her shoulders as if she were dancing.

We made it to the big granite boulders of the breakwater. "I usually walk out to the light at the end. The rocks are fun to walk on," I said.

"Yeah, but it's getting kind of dark. I think we ought to go back."

"Well, but don't you want to see the first stars come out?" I love the purple ending to a day when everything gets dim and still, but Micale was fidgeting uneasily, so I turned around.

We walked over a strip of colored stones in peaceful silence. Suddenly Micale said, "I can't imagine my mother dating anyone."

I couldn't either. That was a good thing about Micale's parents. They were so solid and settled.

"In fact, if you ask me," Micale went on, "I think it's amazing my father and mother ever got together. Unless maybe she asked *him* out. Probably she did. I could see her saying, 'Wesley, you take me to dinner tonight.' Then once he got in the habit of listening to her, she could probably say, 'Wesley, let's get married now.' Dad's pretty easy to convince if you're firm with him." Micale hopped over a rock. "I think having a mother who dates must be fun."

"Well, it isn't," I snapped. "And I'd rather not talk about it."

"You don't have to get mad," she said.

The whole end-of-day calm was shattered. I started stewing about Mom and George again, and I couldn't relax until Mom got home just as Micale and I finished a game of Clue. It was the second gift Micale'd brought me, and I liked it a whole lot better than the spider.

It was humiliating. I started dozing off over Clue, which was the only ordinary gift I'd brought Meg—my mother's selection naturally. I guess all that salt air was corroding my brain, because I couldn't keep my eyes open. Anyway, I went to bed early—probably the first time since crib days that I'd done that voluntarily. Boy did I sleep!

When I woke up, there was Meg asleep in the next bed. She looked about ten years younger without the frown line. After admiring the long lashes resting on her cheeks, I got restless and dug the bubble maker out of my tote bag. Just as an experiment to see if bubbles could wake someone up, I started blowing some her way. Sure enough, one landed on her nose and she opened her eyes to a cloud of rainbow-tinted bubbles. Cute, huh? But did I get a smile?

"Now what are you up to Micale?" she asked without even looking my way. No wonder she and my mother get along. She even sounded like my mother.

"It's your next present," I said. "Don't you love it? Of course you do. Anyone who goes for sunsets has to like bubbles."

Finally, a smile. "You nut," Meg said. It was the nicest thing she'd said to me since I arrived.

When I finished using the bathroom, I found her knee to knee with her mother at the tiny corner table in the kitchen. They both shut up and looked up at me. So guess who they must have been talking about. "Sleep well, Micale?" Heather asked.

"Sure. Did you learn a lot about dips and spreads?"

"No, they canceled the workshop. We just went for a drink and talked."

"Too bad," I said. "Or was it good?"

Heather laughed. "Now I have two of you to report to? Forget it. I'm going to work. Meg will get your breakfast. You two enjoy yourselves." She gave me an equal opportunity kiss after Meg got hers. I'm not much of a kisser, but I liked it from Heather.

I made myself a peanut butter sandwich for breakfast. "So what's the plan for the day?" I asked Meg as I ate.

"Well, low tide's around ten. That's when I've got to check the clam beds. You can come if you want."

"Sure. And then?"

"That'll take most of the morning. Then we can do what you'd like," Meg said.

Fair enough. I figured I'd take a book along for when I got tired of watching her work. She wrote something on a list on the refrigerator door. Later when I looked, it read, "economy-size peanut butter." Good, she'd begun to accept me.

"So what about the kids around here?" I asked her while she was washing up the breakfast dishes.

"Nobody I met in school lives near here. We're on a sort of peninsula called Indian Neck, which is in South Wellfleet. It's mostly summer people and rental cottages. And even the town of Wellfleet, which is bigger, doesn't have enough kids for its own middle school and high school. We get bussed down to Eastham."

"Wow, you're lucky I came," I said. "I mean, with your mother working, you must get really lonely during the day."

"I keep pretty busy," she said, not giving an inch.

The question was, what was *I* going to keep busy with here at the end of the world? "Hey, you know what we could do? We could have a sleep-over party," I said with enthusiasm. I'm always enthusiastic about my own ideas. "Call up some kids you know from school and let their parents drive them over. We could cook hamburgers on the grill and have a bonfire on the beach and—"

Meg was shaking her head. "No bonfires allowed on the beach. And I don't have anybody's phone number. I was only in school here for a little over a month, Micale."

"So? You must have gotten friendly with somebody. You're the all-American girl, Meg. You always have friends." She shook her head. "You mean to tell me you sat in a lunchroom every day for weeks and didn't talk to anybody?"

"Talking to people is different from being friends with them," she said. "Friends take time."

"Oh, yeah?"

"Look, Micale, I'm sorry. We just don't have the kind of fun and games you're looking for here."

"Well, you don't have to get huffy about it," I said.

"I'm not. But you're making me feel bad that I don't know anybody," Meg said.

"I'm sorry. Don't worry. We'll make friends together. That'll be better anyway."

Meg frowned. She looked as if she wanted to say something, but she bit her lip and didn't. "Say it," I said. "Come on. You can tell me what you're thinking. One thing you're going to like about me is, you can tell me anything."

She got a glint in her eyes. "What I was thinking about was your friends. I haven't seen anybody like Orrin or Louray around here."

"No, they're kind of special. They're characters. I like characters. Don't you?"

"Sometimes," she said. She was still being careful with me. Then she said, "Anyway, Mom said she'd drop us in town on her day off so I can show you around. You can look for characters then."

"Good . . . Won't Heather stay with us?"

"No. George is taking her out on his boat."

"And he didn't invite us?"

"No, he didn't."

"Just as well," I said. "Boats make me seasick." Meg had that broody look again. "Is it George you're worried about, or is it you don't want Heather to date anyone?"

Meg teared up again. "I want her to meet somebody nice," she said with feeling.

"How do you know George isn't nice?"

She shrugged and wouldn't look at me. It was the earring, I bet. "You want somebody in a business suit, Meg, right?"

She shook her head. "You don't understand."

"Meg," I said, "it's dumb to worry about an adult. You can't change them. They're already programmed."

"It isn't just the last guy," Meg said. "Mom always picks wrong. She even picked wrong when she married my father."

"How do you know?"

"He deserted us, didn't he? What kind of man is that?"

I'd heard Ma talking about him, that he'd been a teacher in the school and that he'd run off with another teacher when Meg was just a baby. Stuff like that is out of my range. So I wasn't about to give her advice on her father. "Listen," I said, "the point is parents are supposed to take care of *us*. All *we* have to do is get good report cards."

She swallowed and said, "In your house maybe . . . Come on. Let's go do the clam beds."

She got a rake and a basket and heavy leather gloves and told me to wear old sneakers because they'd get mucky on the sand flats. I said I'd go barefoot, but she nixed that. "Your feet'll get all cut up," she said. "Broken shells cut like razors." She looked me up and down. What for, I don't know, since I had on the same clothes as yesterday, but anyway we set off.

The good effect of the bubbles was gone. Meg looked like a walking rain cloud. I wondered if the kid was clinically depressed. My mother was always talking about people being clinically depressed. It means more than just being in a down mood. It's serious stuff. On the other hand, maybe Meg was right to worry. Heather looked pretty easy to hurt. She wasn't cased in steel like my mother.

It was a long walk to the clam flats. I didn't like the beach at low tide all that much. First of all, it smelled fishy, and second of all, if you weren't walking over garbagy seaweed and shell messes, you were squishing through gray muck that oozed over your sneakers. I saw lots of little green crabs. "Do these things bite?" I asked Meg.

"No. I mean, just a nip maybe. But they eat the seed clams. So do the moon snails, and sea gulls. Starfish too. That's why you've got to keep checking the beds so the seed clams won't all get eaten."

"So you're a farm girl," I said. "A shellfish-farm girl."

"I guess so."

She sounded disgustingly cheerful about it. Didn't she know kids are supposed to spend their time playing, not doing hard labor? "You know," I said, "too much sense of responsibility's bad for you."

"So's too little," she snapped back, and gave me that look that would probably drill a hole through my head by summer's end.

We got to the end of the sandy beach. "Here we are," she said.

As far as you could see, out toward what she said was Lieutenant's Island, was mucky, yucky mud flats littered with boxes. The square frames were for growing shellfish Meg told me. Colored markers separated the grants. Her aunt's grant was enormous. I couldn't believe one kid was going to check out all those screened-over seed beds, but she set to work in her high rubber boots and leather gloves as if she knew what she was doing. A whole family was out there on the mud flats a block from shore, working on their grant, and a man in hip boots was loading dripping bags of clams into a truck. It looked like everybody in sight meant business.

Meg said to me, "You could get out the moon snails if you want to help. I'll do the crabs since I have the gloves."

The moon snails were kind of pretty and there weren't that many of them, so I said, "Sure," and took a plastic bag and started helping her. I stuck a few snails in my pocket to keep. They ranged from the size of my fingernail to the size of my palm, and from white to pinkish-gray and tan. I was halfway to nowhere in that emptied-out bay by the time the bag was full. Suddenly I started sinking. I screamed my head off as my foot disappeared into mud, and I imagined the rest of me going under like in some horror movie. Meg came running.

"What's wrong?"

"I'm in quicksand," I yelped.

"No, you're not. It's just soft mud. You won't go under all the way, don't worry."

I was about to argue, but then I realized I'd stopped going down. Now, mind you, I was in up to my ankle. I mean, it was scary. But I did stop sinking, and she gave me her hand and helped me pull my foot out, minus the sneaker. Then she popped my sneaker out of the hole. "Here," she said. "You better go wash this off."

"Yeah, I think I'll take a break," I said. I held up the bag to show her, and she smiled approvingly.

Off duty, I took my wet, muddy sneakers and myself back to the dry dunes and sat down to rest. Everybody was still working. After a while I got restless. I'd forgotten to bring my book. I was not about to volunteer for more moon snail duty, and I certainly wasn't going to have anything to do with those nasty little green crabs. "Nip" she'd said. I bet they nipped!

I climbed up the dune and through somebody's yard. It was a really nice beach house, kind of Japanese-looking with patios around it and a fancy bronze sundial, nothing like Aunt Jane's shack. I walked down the driveway and along the sandy road below it and came out on another road. I followed that for a while and came upon another child laborer. The place seemed to be full of them.

"Hi," I said to the boy sanding away at the fender of a truck, a big truck that had a flat bed and meant business. "You do bodywork?"

"Looks that way," he said. "Except I'm not getting paid for this."

"I know," I said. "Your mother's a trucker and your dad ran away with her best friend, so you're helping her out."

"My mom works in the bank, and my dad's at work in the lumberyard," the kid said to me. "Who are you?"

"Name's Micale. I'm visiting Meg Waters for the summer. You know her? She lives somewhere around here. I don't know exactly where because I'm sort of lost."

"Over the hill and across the gut that way." He pointed, then went back to his sanding. The sound hurt my teeth.

"How come you're repairing the truck?" I asked.

"My dad got permission for me to use it for the Fourth of July parade."

"You're going to drive it?"

"Me? I'm only twelve. That's how I know Meg. We were in the same class."

"Really?" He was kind of cute in a standard

friendly blond sort of way, and he already had some muscles in his arms. "You look older than twelve," I said. I figured he'd like that.

"Yeah, I know," he said, taking it for granted.

"So what's the Fourth of July parade about?"

"It's just a parade. My scout troop's doing a float on Indians, you know the ones that were here, the Wampanoags."

"Really? Need any Wampo—whatever women?"

"No. We're doing a hunting party—all guys. But you could be in the parade if you want. All you got to do is decorate your bike or something, and you can get in."

"I don't have a bike."

"Too bad."

"Well, what else is there?"

"I don't know. The neighborhood associations did things last year. Like the Little People of Long Pond. They had faces painted on kids' middles and big huge hats so they looked like dwarfs or something. It was cool. And the fire truck was in it. And there was a float about women's rights. And the Historical Society had a lot of old-time costumes people dressed up in. And there's always clowns."

"Clowns," I said. "That's it. Any parade can use extra clowns. Who do we see to get in?" I was excited again. This was it. This was the way to the fun house.

He grinned down at me and said he'd find out and call me.

"Well, what's your name?" I asked him.

"Jim Bruder."

I offered to give him Meg's phone number, but he said he'd look it up in the book. "Meg's staying at her aunt's house, right? Whitman's the name, right?"

That was when I realized he had a crush on Meg. Otherwise, why would he remember where she was staying and what her aunt's name was, right? So next I asked him, "Hey, do you ever go swimming?"

"Sure."

"Well, where?"

He looked at me as if I were slow. "There." He pointed. "Off the beach. Oh, sometimes I go to Great Pond, or the ocean. Why?"

I thought fast. "Why" was because I wanted to know where to find him, but what I came up with was, "Do the little green crabs bite?"

He laughed. "They're worse than piranhas," he said. "Eat the flesh off you, and you're dead before you can leave the water."

He was kidding, of course. "Oh, yeah," I said. "Thanks."

"See you," he said, and for the second time went back to work. I let him.

I ambled off, thinking as I went. Some of the stuff I'd brought to give Meg as presents would work as part of the clown outfit. The funny glasses maybe. The face paint. The wigs. I love costumes, especially the kind that disguise you completely.

Fourth of July was a little more than a week off. Good, that gave us just enough time. I was so busy thinking, I got back to Aunt Jane's shack before I knew it. We were going to have fun this summer, Meg and I. I'd teach her to be a kid, and maybe Jim Bruder would help me.

I picked up more green crabs from that clam bed than I thought there could be in the whole bay. By the time I'd filled two bags full of the spidery little things, my back was aching, and I was glad the tide had turned and the water was getting so deep that I had to stop. I hoped I'd rescued enough seed clams so Aunt Jane would still have a crop to harvest in a couple of years. Meanwhile, the problem was getting rid of the crabs. Too bad they couldn't be eaten. I dumped them in a hole some kid had dug in the dry sand, covered them carefully with more sand, and collapsed with my back against the dune.

Micale had gone. She'd probably gotten bored waiting for me. I hoped she wasn't back at the house setting up another practical joke. Micale might be as smart as Mom said, but spiders in the salad was kindergarten stuff. So was bubble blowing. Although waking up to all those bubbles had been kind of nice.

What I really enjoy doing when I'm alone is daydreaming. I like it even better than reading. Today the bay was sparkling and still. I slipped into a daydream about swimming way out where the water was rumpled and an early sailboat was trying to catch some wind. In my dream, the waves start kicking up. I'm having a hard time swimming. A boy sees me struggling. He turns his sailboat into the wind to stop it near me and asks if I want a ride to shore. I climb aboard, and it turns out he lives near Aunt Jane's cottage. In fact, he knows me from school. He asks if I like sailing and offers to give me lessons, and then—

And then I remembered that I'd promised Micale we'd do what she wanted this afternoon. It was time to get myself back to the cottage.

"There you are," Micale said when she saw me. She was stretched out on Aunt Jane's only cushioned lounge chair and was reading in the shade of the house. "You'll never guess who I met this morning."

"King Kong," I said.

"Not bad, not bad at all. Almost funny in fact. I'll give you a hint. It was a boy."

"You met a boy?" I was surprised. "Good for you, Micale."

"No, it's good for you. You're the one he's got a crush on."

"Huh? Nobody's got a crush on me," I said.

"Jim Bruder? Tall, blond, toothy smile and muscles?"

I gasped. Jim was a boy from my class who featured in a lot of my daydreams. But he couldn't have a crush on me! My first day of class, he'd dropped his math homework in the aisle, and I stamped the imprint of my sneaker bottom right over his neat, clean page of numbers. I'd wanted to die. I offered to copy the page over for him, but he said, "Don't worry. No problem." And he smiled at me. After that nothing happened. Absolutely nothing. The most we said to each other during my weeks in his class was hello.

"I guess you like him, huh?" Micale was grinning at me.

I put my hands up to my hot cheeks and said, "Well, he's cute. All the girls like him."

"Oh, yeah? But he likes *you*. He knew where you lived. He knew who you were when I mentioned your name. He even knew your aunt's last name. I bet he looked it up."

Hope blinded me for a few seconds. Then I came to my senses. "Everybody knows who everybody is and where they live around here. It's a small town, Micale."

"You don't believe he could have a crush on you? What's the matter with you? Don't you like yourself?"

"Sure I do, but—"

"But what?" she demanded. "Never mind. You'll get a chance to see for yourself how he feels about you. We're going to be in the Fourth of July parade with him."

"We are?"

"Yup. He's going to be an Indian on some Boy Scout float, and we'll be clowns. I have half the stuff we need already, and I know how to do clown makeup."

"Clowns?" I frowned. "Not me. I'm not making a fool of myself in front of Jim."

"Oh, come on, Meg. Don't be like that. Tell you what. You look good in your swimsuit. We'll hang out on the beach this afternoon so he can see you as a sex object first."

I folded my arms across my chest and told her off. "I do *not* consider myself a sex object, Micale." Then I marched into the kitchen to get some lunch before I lost my temper with her.

Micale followed on my heels. "Jim's going to give me the lady's phone number, the one we have to call about the parade. Come to the beach with me, Meg. Please?"

"I've never seen him on the beach. Not even once, and I swim every day," I said.

"But I know where *he* swims," Micale said.

It was tempting. Instead of watching me stomp on his homework, he'd see me do something I did pretty well. And I do look good in the pink and white striped suit. Could it be that Jim Bruder liked me? I thought of every hello he'd ever given me. They were all stored in my brain. But he'd gone to the eighth-grade ball even though he was only a seventh grader. Some eighth-grade girl had invited him. Of course, that didn't mean she was his girlfriend. Most of the time he hung out with his jock friends—all male. He played basketball and soccer and was friendly to everybody, girls too. No telling who he liked best. Suppose, by some miracle, it was me! The possibility made me giddy.

"Meg, stop thinking and put on your suit," Micale said. "You know you want to."

"I'm not going to be a clown. No way," I said. "I hate doing anything in front of an audience. I'm not setting myself up to be laughed at."

"You know what your problem is? You take yourself too seriously." Micale sounded so cocksure I got annoyed.

"Well," I said, "I care what people think of me and you don't."

"That's because I'm sure of myself and you're not," Micale said.

"What?" I squawked. She was maddening. "Micale, you're acting just like you do in school. You make everybody mad at you when you argue about everything. I told you no, and that's it."

"Well, you don't have to be mean about it."

"I'm not being mean."

"Yes, you are. You're yelling at me."

I gritted my teeth. She was right. I *was* yelling. I'd lost my temper. She'd been here one day and already she'd made me lose my temper. "I'm sorry," I forced myself to say.

She shrugged. "So are we going to see if he's on

the beach? We ought to let him know you don't want to be a clown."

"Why? What does he care?"

"It was his idea. I think he wanted you to be near him in the parade. I mean he said we should walk behind his float. So you better tell him you don't want to."

"It was Jim's idea?"

"Where do you think I learned about the parade?"

I wavered. If he really wanted me there, what would he think of me for not doing it? That I was a bad sport or something. I considered. "Well, let's go down to the beach and see if he's there," I mumbled.

"Sure, if you want to," Micale said casually.

We ate lunch and I got into my suit. "How about you?" I asked Micale. She was still wearing those jeans and that railroad hat. "I could lend you a suit."

"What color?"

"Black. Last year I had a black one, but it's too short for me. You're smaller than me."

"Yeah. Let's see it," she said. My plain black tank suit with little vees of pink over the hips fit her fine. She eyed herself in the mirror and said, as if she were doing me a favor, "Okay, I'll wear it."

When she covered most of her hair and half her face with the railroad cap, I told her she'd look cuter without it. She grinned. "But I'm not supposed to look cute. *You're* the one he's got a crush on. Let's go."

I grabbed two beach towels and followed her. My

heart was pounding. Awkward and ridiculous as I felt, I might as well have been wearing a clown out- fit. We kept walking until we were halfway back to the clam flats. "About here I think," she said. "It's hard to tell without street signs."

The beach was empty except for a family with an infant in a screened crib. They'd come down from one of the fancy cottages on the dunes. "Maybe we shouldn't swim here," I said anxiously. "He'll know we came just because he told you this is where he goes."

"So?"

"So I don't want him to think I'm chasing him, Micale."

"Why not? Don't you want him to know you like him? He sees you here and knows without you say- ing a word. Neat, huh?"

I squirmed, but in a way she was right. And if he really did like me—

"Well, let's talk about the parade while we're waiting," she said.

"We could be Indian squaws, maybe," I suggested.

"No. He says clowns are what they need. It's the easiest thing to be. Don't worry about the costumes. I'll make them while you do your clam thing."

"You're not going to make any costume for me," I said.

"You don't trust me?"

"Micale," I told her earnestly, "I really hate look- ing silly. I really, really despise looking silly."

"You can be a sad clown, okay?"

"White face with flowers on my cheeks, a lady clown."

"No, no. A lady clown wouldn't be funny. You can be a male with a long blond curly wig like Harpo Marx."

"Who?" I said.

"Don't you watch old movies?"

"No."

She told me all about the Marx brothers. They were her favorite comedians. She wanted to model her clown outfit on Groucho Marx. In fact, she was crouched over walking funny with a stick for a cigar in her mouth in imitation of Groucho when Jim Bruder showed up. I was so distracted by Micale's ideas, I'd forgotten we were waiting for him. All the air went out of me when I saw him.

"Hey," he said. "I looked up that lady's telephone number for you, Micale. Too bad I didn't bring it with me. Hi, Meg. How come you're on this part of the beach?"

"We're here because Micale forgot to ask you something," I gasped out.

He smiled his adorable, crooked-toothed smile and asked what she forgot.

"What did I forget?" Micale asked me.

"What?" I echoed like a moron.

"Micale, what'd you forget to ask me?" Jim turned to ask her.

"I don't know," she said, playing dumb although I

just bet she could have thought up something fast enough if she'd wanted to.

"About—about when the Fourth of July parade is," I put in for her.

They both cracked up. Jim laughed so hard he nearly fell over. Micale threw herself onto the sand and howled. When I realized what I'd said, I wanted to bolt for home and hide, but my legs went weak. I just stood there.

"What a sense of humor," Jim said when he stopped laughing. He dropped his towel on the sand and asked what kind of clowns we were going to be.

"Funny ones," Micale said. "Hey, nobody in your family is fat, are they?"

"Why?"

"Well, you know, extra-big pants."

"There's a store in town that sells used clothing cheap. Maybe you could find stuff there," Jim suggested.

"Great," Micale said. "Want to come shopping with us?"

"Shopping? Me? No way," he said. "Anybody ready for a swim?" He started walking toward the water.

"Meg is," Micale said and shoved me after him.

We walked into the water side by side, Jim Bruder and me. And it wasn't a daydream either. It was really happening.

"So how does your mother like working for George?" Jim asked me.

"Fine, I guess. You know him?"

"Yeah. George's a neat guy. He's going to give me a job when I'm old enough—if he's still in business. I helped him do some bodywork on his truck, just a little touch-up . . . That guy's had some life!"

"You think he's done all the things he says?" I asked.

"Before he got married, sure. Then his wife took over his life. That's what he told me. It's kind of hard to believe, I mean, that he'd let her. But I guess she was a very bossy lady. It's probably just as well she dumped him . . . Hey, race you." He splashed into deeper water and dove in.

I looked back at Micale and called, "You coming in?"

"Me? Don't worry about me," she said. "Just do your thing." She winked at me. Jim was already halfway across the bay. Instead of trying to catch up, I did my regular back-and-forth laps parallel to shore. He was out of the water, already dry, and talking to Micale when I finished.

"Why don't you guys swim here again tomorrow? I'll bring my Aerobie and we can toss it around," he said. He looked at me.

I was wringing the water out of my hair. He wanted us to come back tomorrow? Maybe Micale was right and he did like me, not as much as I liked him probably, but even if he just *liked* me that was great. "Sure," I said breathlessly. "We'll come back tomorrow."

I was so excited that on the way home I had to talk about Jim. "Isn't he something?" I asked Micale.

"Nice guy, yeah," Micale said.

"I can't believe he wants to see us again."

"You, you mean. He asked you," Micale said.

"Me." I beamed at her. Mom had been right. Micale was basically a good kid despite the plastic spiders in the salad and the rest. She'd brought me and Jim Bruder together. No friend of mine had ever done anything nicer for me than that.

CHAPTER

SEVEN

MICALE

My jeans stunk. There was no way to get around it. They stunk. "I guess they must need a washing," I said when I picked them up to put on Saturday morning. Meg looked at me with such disgust, I said, "Honest, I didn't do anything in them."

"They smell as if you did," Meg said.

I took it as a good sign that she'd stopped being polite. It meant she'd accepted me. Unless it meant she couldn't stand me and didn't mind hurting my feelings. But hopefully she was liking me now. That would show my mother. I couldn't be so bad if Meg the Perfect liked me. Maybe we'd end up close as sisters. I've always wanted a sister. Friends come and go, but sisters are there when you want a game of go fish, right?

Meg led me to the washing machine and told me to be sure to shut the water faucets off after I used it. "In case the hoses burst," she explained. Then she added, "You better empty your pockets." I did and we discovered the moon snails. How was I supposed to know those pretty shells had live animals inside that would smell when they died? We dumped the snails into the garbage.

"Let's go wake up Heather," I said next. I was eager to get to that store that had the old clothes. Actually, I was just eager to get to town.

"If George didn't have that plumbing problem, Mom would be working. She usually works Saturdays. This is her one chance to sleep in," Meg, the mother guardian, told me.

We went back to wrangling about the clown outfits. I'd given her my next present, which was the weird glasses with the goggly eyes. She wanted to make them part of the costume because they'd disguise her, but I'd changed my mind about the glasses. "Real clown makeup is better," I told her. "Believe me, no one's going to recognize you. Besides, you said you barely know anybody in town." She looked doubtful. Then I hit her with the idea of acting goofy and playing tricks on one another as we walked along in the parade.

"Never," Meg said. "Forget that. I'm not putting down a banana peel for you to slip on, and I'll kill you if you do it to me. I mean it, Micale. And no water balloons and no squirting flowers and no embarrassing noises either."

"So what do you want to do? Just poke along behind the Boy Scout truck in baggy clothes? What's the point of being a clown if you don't make people laugh?"

"You're sure Jim said clowns are all they need?"

I blew out my lips at her with sound effects and some unplanned spit. If she ever found out Jim hadn't exactly suggested we be clowns, and that we could have just rented some bikes and decorated them and ridden behind the Boy Scout float in normal clothes, she *would* kill me. "You know, I haven't seen the pier where the parade's going to start from yet either," I said to distract her.

"What's that got to do with anything?"

"Well, I might like the pier. Let's wake Heather up and go."

"You won't like the pier," Meg said. "It's got nothing but boats."

"No game parlors? No shooting galleries? Nothing?"

"Wednesday nights in July and August they hold square dances on it," Meg said. Her eyes widened dreamily. "I wonder if Jim goes."

"Square dancing? Ask him."

"I couldn't do that, but you and I could go, and if he was there—"

"I'll ask him," I said.

"Micale, no!"

I grunted impatiently. Frankly, I was pretty bored with Jim. After chasing an Aerobie around with him, and watching him and Meg swim, I could easily imagine him grown-up with two kids and a mortgage. In male types, I go for weird and unpredictable.

While the washing machine was doing its thing, I let Meg talk me into opening my suitcase. Ever since my mother had called when I wasn't around and asked Meg how my new pants fit me, Meg had been curious. "I don't see how you can have new clothes and not want to wear them," she said.

"I hate new clothes."

"That's abnormal," she told me.

"Meaning I'm different from you."

She thought it over, then nodded. "I guess that's what I do mean. You're *so* different from me, Micale."

I gave Meg credit for reconsidering her opinions. Most people won't. Also she'd been pretty decent to cover for me by not telling my mother I hadn't touched the suitcase yet. See, Ma had made me promise that if the pants didn't fit I'd send them back so she could return them. Most of the clothes she buys for me get returned. You'd think she'd give up, but not her.

I was yanking stuff out of the suitcase and complaining to Meg, "Clothing's such a waste of time— deciding what you need, buying it, figuring out what to wear with what, sticking it into drawers, deciding when it's dirty. It uses half your life up."

I stopped when I heard Meg's "Oooo." She'd picked up this fleecy pastel top I'd dropped on the floor. "Oooo, this is so pretty. You could wear it to town, Micale."

"You wear it if you like it so much," I said. It ticked me off to see her more enthused about the top than about any of the neat presents I'd given her. She was staring at it with the dopey glazed expression she gets when she sees Jim.

"I'll just try it on," she said.

I could tell by the way she looked at herself in the mirror that she loved that top. "It's yours," I said. "It's too fluffy for me."

"I can't keep it." Meg frowned. "I could wear it today, but then you have to take it back."

"Why?"

"Because your mother bought it for you, not me. And she must've spent plenty on it."

"So what? She bought it on sale and can't return it."

"Maybe you'll change your mind and like it," Meg said. I started to argue with her, but she got teary eyed and told me if I wouldn't take it back, she wouldn't keep it on. Then I had a hard time getting her to wear it even for the day.

Heather finally came out of her bedroom all puffy-faced and mumbly. Meg coaxed her awake with coffee and oatmeal.

"Let's skip the clam beds today," Heather said.

"Then the crabs'll take over again," Meg objected.

"All right." Heather yawned. "I'll do them. When's low tide?"

"Around noon."

"Good. Then I have time to go back to sleep."

Meg looked at me. "Mom," she said, "can't you

take us to town today? Micale hasn't seen Wellfleet yet."

"Oh, right." Heather smiled at me apologetically. "I'm sorry, Micale. I'll get ready and take you now. I need to go food shopping anyway."

I liked the town. First came a rowboat filled with red petunias that split the two main streets. Main Street had the old white-clapboard New England town hall and the shops with the cutesy names. Commercial Street had art galleries and a lumberyard. Commercial Street was also neat because of the marsh behind it and the Victorian guest houses. It ended at the pier where there were a lot of boats, some real fishing boats—trawlers or something that Meg seemed to think were special—and wonder of wonders, a soft-ice-cream stand. We bought frozen yogurts even though it was eleven o'clock. Heather doesn't worry about things like spoiling your lunch. Ma would have had a fit.

"Okay if I leave you kids off on Main Street and pick you up in a couple of hours?" Heather said. She was looking very perky.

"You're in a good mood," I observed.

"Why not? I have the day off and it's not raining and George is taking me for a ride in his Boston whaler after the plumber leaves."

"Oh, right," Meg said without enthusiasm.

"Poor guy hasn't had his boat out since he bought it. He's giving me a tour of the harbor."

"So you'll only be gone about an hour?" Meg asked.

"Ummm, I think more. George is in need of a shoulder to unload on."

"Unload what on?" I asked.

"Oh, you know. He was married for twenty-seven years and now he's divorced, and his children make excuses and don't come to see him, and that worries him a lot."

"Married for twenty-seven years? He must be pretty old," Meg said.

Heather considered. "He married young."

"But you're just in your thirties," Meg said, "and George has gray hair."

Heather laughed. "Stop worrying, love. So far George and I are only friends."

"I thought he was your boss," Meg said. "Can't he talk to you at work? You're supposed to be free when you get a day off, like to do something fun with your daughter."

"Meg, you have Micale. Don't be difficult."

Meg frowned. "Just don't wear your new bathing suit, okay?"

"The one I bought when I got yours? Why not?"

"Mom, it shows too much, and you're going to be alone in the boat with that man."

"I'll wear a shirt. Really, Meg, you can trust me."

"But what about him?"

"Tell you what. I'll bring George home for supper so you can see what a pussycat he is."

"No thanks," Meg said quickly. "I believe you."

After Heather left, I said to Meg, "You ought to let her bring him home. You might even like him."

Meg snorted. "Probably I will the first time. They work hard to make you like them at the beginning."

A.I.M. was the name of the used clothing place. It was between a stationery store and a gift shop, and they didn't have just clothing. They had toys and glasses and dishes and books and a dressmaker's dummy and jewelry. The first thing I found was a bin of wild-colored boxer shorts. One pair even had pink elephants on it. I snatched up that one and a pair of red shorts with black valentine hearts that were sort of big, but could be taken in.

"You're not going to buy *those* things!" Meg said in disgust.

"They're gorgeous," I said, "and they're only a quarter apiece." Then I found these wonderful balloony farmer's jeans with suspenders and very short legs. "Perfecto," I said. "What a place this is!"

Meg followed after me, making faces at everything I liked, including the big straw hat with a filmy scarf that I said I could use on the beach.

"You wouldn't!"

"Well, you don't like my railroad cap," I said.

I bought a beach jacket with Mexican appliqués. It was an amazingly hideous poison-green, sort of the color of Meg's face by the time I opened my little leather purse and dug out the cash for my treasures.

"Waste of money," Meg grumbled. "You don't need all that stuff for your clown outfit."

"Want to bet?"

"What are you going to do, wear them all at once?"

"Some of them are for you."

"Me!" she yelled so loud people in the store turned to look at us. "You think I'm going to wear any of those things? NEVER."

I tut-tutted and said, "You sure use that word a lot, Meg."

We went outside and found Heather waiting at the curb in the pickup with the week's food supply in bags in the back. "What's the matter?"

"Nothing," Meg said. She hitched herself into the truck and sat between her mother and me looking grim.

"Did you find what you were looking for in there?" Heather asked.

"Did we ever," I said just as Meg said, "Not me."

"Meg's afraid of acting silly in public," I said.

"Meg's never acted silly," Heather said. "She was even a solemn baby."

"I hate being laughed at, and I don't want Jim to see me as a clown," Meg cried. I mean she really cried with tears and all.

"But, Meg," Heather said, "even if he sees you in a clown outfit, he'll still think you're pretty."

"I'm *not* pretty."

"Of course you are," Heather said.

"My eyes are too close together," Meg said. "And my bones are too big."

"You're attractive," Heather said. "You have healthy, outdoor good looks."

"Micale's the one who's pretty. Anyway, without her awful hats she would be," Meg said stubbornly. "I'm just big." But she wiped her tears away and simmered down as Heather drove us home. I thought the storm was over, which just showed how much I still had to learn about Meg.

EIGHT

MEG

Mom was starting again. I just knew it. It was all those old movies she watched where the guy smiles at the poor girl and dances her off to live happily ever after. The first thing Mom told me about the one that beat her up was what a great smile he had. Now she's got George. And he has a smile, too.

"So how do I look?" Micale asked. I was at the sink, cleaning up after lunch. Micale stood in the doorway to the kitchen in the elephant shorts she'd bought at the thrift shop that morning. They showed over the top of the baggy jeans, which only stayed on her because of the suspenders.

"Like a clown," I said. Her black wig had come out of that tote bag of hers along with the fake nose and the false mustache. The wig had tufts of hair sticking out in all directions. Maybe it was my grim mood, but Micale's weird ideas of what to pack for vacation made me wonder if she was normal.

"Well, is it funny? Why aren't you laughing? Ha-ha," Micale encouraged me, as if maybe I didn't know how.

"Ha-ha," I said.

"How about like this?" Micale did her bent-over Groucho Marx imitation, but with a bubble pipe instead of a cigar.

"Okay, I guess."

"What's with you?" she asked. "Look, if it's depressing you that much, you don't have to be a clown. I'll think of something else for you."

"What? The back end of a donkey? No, I'll do it. I said I'd do it and I'll do it."

"Wow, what enthusiasm!"

"It's not the parade, Micale."

"Then what?" She hopped up on the table and leaned toward me. "Come on, tell me. I'm really a great listener, and maybe I can help."

"I just don't want Mom to get involved with her boss," I burst out.

"You want her to find someone in a business suit who looks like a grown-up Jim Bruder, right?"

I nodded. Jim grown-up would be a solid kind of guy.

"I didn't see any business suits in Wellfleet, did you?" Micale asked.

"It's not how he looks. It's how he is. I want someone who'll take care of her and love her, not a guy who'll take advantage of her again."

"What do you mean 'again'?" Micale asked. "Were there other losers before the last guy?"

Other losers? There had been a string of them. One disappeared right after Mom made a big Christmas dinner for him, and two turned out to be married, and a few just decided not to take on a wife and ready-made child. The saddest part was that Mom never learned. She still expected each guy to be her hero, although she *has* stopped promising to find me a father. I've finally convinced her that I'm too grown-up now to know what to do with one, and that I don't feel deprived having just her. But how could Micale understand? Her parents are so solid and safe. I shook my head and didn't answer her.

"You know what we could do?" Micale lit up with her new idea. "Before Heather falls for George, we could run an investigation on him. Find out what kind of guy he really is."

"An investigation? Who'd answer a kid's questions about an adult?"

"Jim Bruder might. He knows George."

I perked up. She was right. Besides, I was glad of any excuse to see Jim. "So what should we do? Try the beach?" I asked.

"Let's go to his house," Micale said.

"Oh, no. I couldn't do that."

"Why?"

"Well, what if his mother came to the door? And besides, he'll think I'm chasing him."

"Okay," Micale said. "Get me his number and I'll call him up."

I stared at her. She was so bold! Nothing frightened Micale when it came to people. Finally, I looked up the number and held my breath while she dialed it. She sounded perfectly normal asking to speak to Jim, but then she said, "Oh, well thanks," and hung up.

"He's out?" I asked, starting to breathe again.

"He went fishing with his father down at the breakwater. Let's go."

"Are you nuts? His father's with him."

"So? We're only going to ask Jim something."

The tide was so high that hardly any beach was left to walk on. We had to go by road. It was a cool, cloudy day, the kind where it might rain but then again it might not. Micale was complaining about walking. "It has to be bad for you because it's no fun," she said. "Anything that's no fun has to be bad for you."

She sounded so positive it annoyed me. "Life isn't all about having fun," I told her.

"Sure it is, so long as you don't hurt anybody."

I studied Micale's face. It sparkled with life. For a minute I wished I were like her and could just act without thinking about the consequences. I get knotted up in worry about what people will think of me. She couldn't care less. But would I really want to be like her? I'd never know, because there was no way that I could be.

I walked along, plucking at the ragged ends of my old long-sleeved dark-blue sweatshirt, wishing I'd thought to put on something better. I could have worn Jim's favorite color—if I'd known what that was, but I didn't. If I had Micale's nerve, I'd just come right out and ask him.

When we got near the breakwater, I spotted Jim with the other fishermen lined up along the big rocks and started hiccuping from excitement.

"Hey, Jim, catch anything?" Micale yelled.

"A couple of blues," he told her.

We went closer and Micale said hello to his father while I held my breath to get rid of the hiccups. Micale crouched to study the teeth on the blues. "Yikes, do those things swim close to shore?" she asked.

"Sometimes," Jim said. "I know a fellow lost a big toe to one. Blues'll bite at anything." He winked at me as he tried to scare her.

"Don't listen to him," his father said. "You want to go swimming, go. So long as you stay close to shore, your toes are safe."

"You know George who has the sandwich shop?" Micale asked, getting right down to business. "We were wondering about him. Do you know where he comes from?"

Mr. Bruder must have thought Micale was asking him because he was the one who answered. "Told me he comes from Chicago," he said as he reeled in his line. He whipped his rod back and flipped it so the lure flew way out into the bay before sinking below the lippy gray waves. "George ran a restaurant there with his wife. Only been in Wellfleet once on vacation, he told me, but here's where he picked to come when she threw him out. Guess that must've been a good vacation."

"He a friend of yours?" Micale asked.

"I wouldn't say as he's a friend. I know him from when he comes by the lumberyard. He's fixing up his place."

"The sandwich shop?" Micale asked.

"No, the old house he bought in the hollow by Route 6."

"That's his house, Dad? Where they used to keep horses?" Jim asked.

"Yeah."

"Seems like a big place for one man," Jim said.

"Well, he planned on having his kids staying with him."

"But they don't come," Micale said.

"I wouldn't know," Mr. Bruder said.

He knew more than my mother knew though, more than she'd told me anyway. "Does George have a temper?" I asked, thinking of Mom's last boyfriend.

Mr. Bruder glanced at me in surprise. "I wouldn't know," he said again. "But he's Greek. Papandoulos. Them Greeks can be pretty hot-blooded." His pole tipped down. "Strike," he said and turned his attention to the fish he'd hooked.

"You going swimming today?" Micale asked Jim.

"I already swam," Jim said, grinning at her. "How about you, Micale? You going to risk putting your toe in?"

"Not me," she said. "Not with all those crabs and bluefish."

I was thinking about that after we said good-bye and started walking home. "You aren't really afraid of going in the water, are you?" I asked her when we were out of earshot.

"Hey, everybody's afraid of something." She began dancing backward, facing me as I walked. "So what do you think about George now?"

"Well, you found out a lot, but we don't know why his wife dumped him, and we don't know why his kids don't come to see him. That's the kind of stuff I need to find out. And who's going to tell us?"

"Let's go look his house over," Micale said.

"What?"

"You can tell something about people by how they live," she said.

"You'd go prowl around somebody's house? Micale!"

"As long as he's out on the bay with your mother, it's safe." She laughed. "You go swimming in the bay with those wicked crabs and man-eating fish, don't you?" She showed her teeth in imitation of the blues and shuddered.

I smiled. Then I laughed out loud. But she was serious. She really was afraid of crabs and bluefish.

"How do we get to the hollow by Route 6?" she asked.

"Walk," I said. "From here it's a couple of miles past our house and up Pilgrim Springs Road."

She groaned and was talking about doing it some other day when a car honked at us. Mrs. Ryan stuck her freckled face out the window of her station wagon. "Hi, girls, need a lift somewhere?" Billie's curly brown ears and sheep face promptly squeezed in beside hers.

"Oh, do we ever!" Micale said.

"Get in," Mrs. Ryan offered, "if you don't mind having Billie all over you."

It was hard to see anything with Billie sitting on my leg, using me as a seat so she could lick Micale's face. But considering how skittish the dog is, I felt honored to be trusted even with her rear end.

"Here you are," Mrs. Ryan said. We thanked her and got out from under Billie. Mrs. Ryan honked good-bye and took off.

"And now to case the joint," Micale said as she stared down the sandy road into the hollow.

I followed her warily. The house was big, but sort of neglected-looking. Someone had started painting the window frames and stopped. A half-collapsed shed was leaning against the side of the house, and weeds surrounded the rest of it. Fences around the horse paddocks were falling down, too. Through the front window we saw a nice-looking dining room, but it didn't have any furniture. In the living room, a couch and chairs were lined up around the walls so that the center looked like an empty stage. I didn't see any books but lots of tapes and a tape player and a big T.V.

We went around back and looked into the kitchen, which was pretty messy with newspapers and mail all over the table and pots on the stove and dishes on the drainboard. "He's not very neat," I said.

"What do you want?" Micale said. "He's got the place set up for himself, everything within reach, and it looks pretty clean."

"But not very nice."

"So he's no interior decorator."

I sighed. "But I still don't know anything about him, Micale."

"Nothing bad, you mean. You should let your mother invite him for dinner. That way we can examine him up close."

I knew she was right, but we walked most of the way home before I could make myself give in. I didn't want to let Mom invite George over. I didn't want to encourage her. On the other hand, how else would I find out if she was getting involved with another loser? All right then. I'd even offer to cook the dinner—that is, if Mom sounded as if she'd had a good time with George on his boat, I would.

Meanwhile, I ought to learn to relax and chat with Jim like Micale did. If I was livelier with him, he might like me better. Micale's fears caused less of a problem than mine. You could avoid crabs and bluefish by not going into the water, but you couldn't avoid people.

CHAPTER

NINE

MICALE

It made me squirmy watching Meg and her mother smooching on the patio before dinner. Not that they were showing off. They're just naturally affectionate toward each other. But I felt odd because Ma and I don't touch each other if we can help it. Or I don't touch her. I even ducked her kiss at the bus station. And there were Heather and Meg sitting with their arms around each other while Heather told us about her ride in the Boston whaler. It's probably because Heather's so young she could practically be Meg's sister. My mother never looked young even when she was. In a high school class photo, she looks like a prison guard. I wondered if having a hard-nosed mother made me a deprived child. Not quite. Jealous was all I was. I was dripping green with jealousy.

"George doesn't know anything but full throttle," Heather was saying. "My bottom's sore from bouncing over the waves. But it was fun. The town looks so different from the water."

"So what did you talk about?" Meg asked.

"Not much. We couldn't hear ourselves think over that engine noise."

"I thought he wanted to cry on your shoulder," Meg said.

"Did I say that? Well, I had him wrong. George doesn't go around feeling sorry for himself. He's too high-spirited."

I waited for Meg to ask more questions. When she didn't, I took over. "Are you going to invite him to dinner some night?" I asked Heather.

"Ummm, some night." Heather sipped the fruit punch Meg had mixed up, made a face and put her glass down. I guess she didn't like the extra sugar I'd added to it.

"How about this week?" I suggested.

"Oh, not this week. I'm invited to his place for his mussel stew on Wednesday. That's his day off. Thursday's mine. If it's a nice day I'll take you girls swimming on the ocean side for a change."

Heather asked how the clown costumes were coming, and I was telling her when the phone rang. My mother. I could see Heather and Meg talking to each other out on the patio from the kitchen where I was standing at the phone.

"Are you behaving yourself?" was Ma's first question.

"I have to," I said. "There's no way for me to get in trouble here."

"You'll find a way, I'm sure," Ma said.

"Ma, instead of insulting me, how about telling me how the grandma's doing."

"Remarkably well. She had two of her friends in and we played bridge yesterday afternoon. And she's wiping me out at gin rummy every evening."

"Do you hug and kiss each other?"

"What?"

"Affection," I said. "You know what that is? Do you and the grandma—"

"We're not a physically affectionate family, Micale. Why?"

"Just asking. So do you miss me a lot?"

She hesitated, because what could she say when she didn't miss me at all? "I miss you some," Ma lied.

"Well, I miss you and Grandma. Tell her, huh? Tell her I asked about her."

"You can talk to her yourself," Ma said.

A click and clatter later there came the grandma's buzzy voice. "How are you, darling?"

"Fine, and you?"

"Getting better faster than the doctors expected. Having your mother around's good for me."

"Did you hug her a lot when she was a kid?"

"Of course," the grandma said. Note: she's been known to say with conviction whatever she wants to be true.

"Well, was she a lovey-dovey mama to me when I was a baby?"

"You never held still long enough to cuddle, if

that's what you mean, Micale. Your mother did the best she could with you."

"So it's all my fault?"

"What is?" Grandma sounded confused.

"Nothing." I got teary eyed. It must be catching. Teary-eyed was Meg not me. "Let me talk to Ma . . . please," I added. The grandmother's big on "pleases" and wasn't likely to pass the receiver along until I remembered the password.

"Micale, what's wrong with you?" Ma demanded.

"Nothing. I'm fine," I said.

"You and Meg are getting along?"

"Sure, we're good pals."

"Is that so? She doesn't mind your warped sense of humor?"

"She's getting used to it. And I'm teaching her to lighten up. Meg's a gloomy Gus, not a smiler like me."

"Really? She never seemed gloomy in school."

"Did the grandma like my funny card?"

"She said it was just like you . . . Are you picking up after yourself?"

"I'm even doing my own wash." That reminded me that my jeans were still in the washing machine. "You wouldn't recognize me, I'm so helpful."

"It sounds too good to be true . . . And how are the new clothes I bought you?"

"Okay. Can I give Meg anything I don't want?"

A deep sigh. "I can imagine what that means. All right. She probably deserves them for putting up with you."

"Listen, Ma," I said. "I know you don't want me to get a swelled head, but I'd appreciate a compliment once in a while instead of the ever-ready put down, you know?"

Silence. "I'll take that under consideration," Ma said. "All right. I'm glad you're behaving yourself."

"Yeah, thanks, you too," I said and hung up. Meg and her mother were getting dinner ready in the kitchen. I went to put my jeans into the dryer. Then I went to our bedroom and dumped all the clothes in my suitcase onto Meg's bed.

"Dinner," Meg called.

"You should have waited for me to set the table," I said.

Heather and Meg exchanged a look, like "Who does she think she's kidding?" and we sat down to eat the chicken salad.

"So when are we having George for dinner?" I asked.

"I don't think Meg wants him here," Heather said.

"Well, if you like him so much, I guess I ought to meet him," Meg said.

"Oh?" Heather beamed. "Really? Lovely. Let's do it next week then. I bet you're going to like George, Meg."

"I hope so," Meg said and shut up again.

"If he's such a great guy, how come his wife doesn't want him?" I asked Heather.

She frowned at me, like what right did I have to ask personal questions, and she said, "I expect he'll tell me someday."

"Does he like kids?" I asked next.

"I think so," Heather said. "He's a real people person."

"Well, I mean, what about his own kids. Does he talk about them?" I asked.

"Micale—" Heather was hesitating on the brink of telling me it was none of my business, which is what my mother would have said as soon as I opened my mouth. But instead, Heather asked me, "How do you know George has children?"

"You said he did. And we met somebody who says George bought a big house here because he wanted his children to come live with him."

"Live with him? But they're grown-up. One lives in Chicago and the other lives in Detroit. Although—who knows?"

"Delicious chicken salad," I said, picking the olives out of it. I don't like green stuff in food either so I picked out the celery, which reminded me of my next gift to Meg. I left mother and daughter to do the dishes and went to dig it out of my tote bag. It looked just like toothpaste, like the brand the Waters used in fact, but it would turn your teeth green— temporarily—when you brushed with it. I left it in the bathroom.

The dishes were done when I got back. "You should have waited. I was going to help," I said. Another exchange of knowing looks. Probably I wasn't the most helpful guest they'd ever had.

"I'm going to take a warm bath," Heather said. "If George calls, tell him I'll call back."

"She likes him a lot already," Meg said glumly after the door to the bathroom closed. "And we know more about him than she does."

"He sounds like a nice guy so far," I offered.

"We'll see."

I got one of my electrifying ideas. "Hey, Meg, let's stake out his house when she's there for dinner."

"Spy on them?"

"Why not? We could sit in the bushes on that hill behind his house and see right into his dining room."

"That's disgusting. I'm not spying on my own mother," Meg said.

"You don't want to protect her?" I shrugged. "Suit yourself. If you think she can defend herself if he comes on to her—well—"

That got Meg. She shuddered and burst out with, "I wish she wouldn't rush into things. Why can't she let *me* pick her boyfriends?"

I had to chuckle. "You're sort of young to be her mother," I said.

"Well," Meg defended herself. "At least I'm objective."

"Sure you are," I mocked her. She tossed her head and went off to our bedroom.

"What's this?" she wanted to know when she saw the stuff piled on her bed. "You moving into my side of the room, Micale?"

"No. That's for you, if you want it. Ma says you deserve it for putting up with me."

"I can't take all these things. They're new." She sounded horrified.

"Yeah, well, anything *old* of mine isn't even worth making rags of, or so my mother says."

"No," Meg said.

"No, what?"

"No, I can't take anything else from you. Thanks, anyway."

"Why not?" I asked. "Listen, I'm not going to wear any of it, and you could use some new clothes. I mean, you *like* clothes and you barely have any."

Meg stiffened and grew six inches. "My mother gives me everything I need," she said.

"I know she tries," I said. "But she can't earn much being an office aide or working in a sandwich shop, Meg. So—"

Meg turned and walked out on me. Whoops, my big mouth again! I followed on her heels, talking as fast as I could to calm her down. "Listen, Meg. You've got a sweetheart of a mother. You're lucky to have her. Believe me, I'd be happy to change places with you. Anyway, it'd be easy for me because all I need's one pair of jeans and a jar of peanut butter."

She marched right out of the cottage and slammed the door in my face. I figured the smartest thing to do was to let her calm down. She'd come back eventually. Meanwhile, I returned to the bedroom and shoved my mother's purchases back in the suitcase where they could stay until I went home, for all I cared. Too bad Meg's pride had gotten in the way. She'd have really enjoyed some of those clothes.

About an hour later I was lying on my bed, reading. Heather came out of the bathroom, which is right opposite our bedroom. She was wearing a robe and nightgown. "Hi, honey," she said to Meg, who was out of my sight. "I'm sorry I was in there so long. I guess I fell asleep in the tub. It's all yours now."

"Thanks, Mom," Meg said, and she went into the bathroom without telling her mother anything about the clothes.

Good, I thought. That must mean she'd forgiven me. Heather stuck her head in to blow me a good-night kiss before she went to her room. I was wondering if either of them brushed their teeth before they went to bed when I heard a scream. Heather bounced out of her bedroom and rushed into the bathroom, leaving the door wide open so I could see Meg standing at the sink naked with her toothbrush in her hand.

"My teeth," Heather said to her. "Do they look green to you?"

"Yes," Meg said. "What'd you eat?"

"Nothing. I was just brushing my hair and—eeek! Your teeth are getting green, too."

I hid my laughter behind the book when Meg marched into our bedroom. "Micale, what'd you do?"

"Me?" I asked innocently.

Meg flashed her green teeth at me and I cracked up. Well, she looked too funny.

"The toothpaste," Heather said from the doorway. "It's the toothpaste, Meg. It's not our regular brand. It's—"

"More of Micale's practical jokes," Meg said with enough disgust to bury me in it.

They calmed down after I showed them that the stuff brushed right off with regular toothpaste. "How about we use green teeth as part of our clown costumes, Meg?" I said.

"No way." Meg was brushing vigorously. "And if you keep this up, you can be in that parade by yourself."

I tiptoed away to give her time to recover, but when we were both in bed with the light out, I asked, "So are you mad at me forever?"

"I should be."

"But you're not?"

"How many more practical jokes are in that tote bag, Micale?"

"Not many."

"Well, don't use the rest, and I'll stop being mad at you."

"Okay," I said meekly. She turned over to go to sleep. "Meg?"

"What?"

"At least I'm not boring."

I didn't get any answer to that one. Didn't she like me anymore? I turned the light on. "Hey," I said, "I was just trying to cheer you up."

She was crying. I saw her shoulders heave. "What's wrong?" I asked. "You hate me?"

"You're just making everything harder," she said.

"With your mother? Or are you still upset about the clothes?"

"It's no fun not having any money, Micale. Believe me, it's no fun."

"I'm sorry," I said. "Me and my big mouth. Really, I'm sorry, Meg. I really, really am."

"Oh, go to sleep," she said.

So I'd learned another thing about her. She didn't hold grudges. That was good. I make friends pretty easily, but lots of times I say something or do something that people won't forgive me for. The worst of it is not knowing what I did. Oh, I ask, but usually they won't tell me. Well, anyone the least bit original in this world is sure to have a hard time. Nobody appreciates us—at first.

CHAPTER

TEN

MEG

That Micale! Never mind treating her like a guest. She was a demon and I had to stop letting her talk me into things. Her and her green toothpaste. And that business with the clothes! Mom's never earned much, but she's always managed to support us, and we don't need charity. Sure, I'd like it if Mom could buy me what Mrs. Elder buys Micale, but she can't, and I don't exactly go around in rags. I'm not Cinderella, no matter what Micale thinks.

Sunday Mom offered to drop us off at Great Island for a half-day hike with a National Seashore ranger. She knew it was something I'd been wanting to do since we'd come. Micale said she didn't feel like it. I was glad about that. I needed to get away from her for a while. But when I said, "Well, I'm going," Micale looked surprised.

"You're going to leave me here alone all day?"

"It's a half-day hike," I said and added hopefully, "You could read."

She went with me. The first thing she did was march up to the ranger, who was waiting for us in his hard-brimmed hat and gray-green uniform, and demand, "What's there to see on this hike?"

"Well," he said, "shorebirds maybe, and crabs and suchlike creatures."

She squinched her face and said, "Yuck." One of the adults gathered there for the five-mile hike along the bay beach to the tip at Jeremy Point snickered. Another one raised an eyebrow.

As soon as we began walking, the ranger started rambling on to whoever stayed close enough to hear him about barrier islands and the fragile dunes and how the sea is constantly changing everything. Micale asked him why the scallop shells were so many different colors, and he explained that it depended on what was in the water where they grew. Like, dark mud made them black. I thought that was interesting, but Micale got bored, or tired, and trailed behind the group. I wasn't surprised when she dropped out about a mile into the walk. Hiking on sand's not that easy.

"What are you going to do?" I asked her.

"Go back," she said. "I'll see you in the parking lot."

I hesitated, wondering if I should go with her. Then I asked myself, what for? She could take care of herself perfectly well. I hurried to catch up with the group. But it was hard to enjoy the hike because I kept thinking about Micale stuck out alone on the empty beach without a tree or any kind of shelter from the hot sun. We each had a bottle of water with us, so she wasn't going to dehydrate or anything, but still, Micale didn't even have a tan to protect her. Pain that she was, I was still responsible for her here as long as my mother wasn't around.

A half an hour later, I finally gave up fighting my conscience and left the group to hustle back to her. I found her, still half a mile from the parking lot, sitting under a beach umbrella, drinking soda and listening to a boom box with a couple of little kids whose parents were fishing. Luckily nobody else was on the beach for a mile in either direction, so the music they were blasting the air with could only bother the birds.

"Did you get bored, too?" Micale yelled at me over the noise. "Want a soda?"

"No thanks. I'll wait for you in the parking lot."

I was angry. She'd messed up the hike for me, and who knew if I'd get another chance at it. I wished I'd just done my thing instead of worrying about her. I wished our mothers hadn't stuck us together for the summer. Micale and I were going to end up hating each other. Sitting on a dune above the parking lot, I simmered and stewed about everything that was wrong in my life. It didn't help that I had a long, dull wait until Mom arrived, and then another wait until Micale showed up.

Monday we woke up to see an ocean of dishwater-colored rain coming down. We'd skipped the clam beds yesterday, and I had to do them. Low tide was after one. I hoped the rain would let up by then.

Micale took one look out the window and said, "I know! Call up Jim and invite him over for a game of hearts or Monopoly or something."

"You call him if you want him," I said firmly.

"You're the one who likes him," she said. Since I wouldn't budge, that was the end of that idea.

After breakfast, Micale curled up on the couch. She read while I vacuumed and dusted and wondered how she could be so lazy. But then she suggested we make cookies, and we did that together. It's hard to stay angry at someone as cheerful as Micale, especially when she's too thick-skinned to even realize I'm mad at her. We had a good time making cookies. Then when the rain let up, Micale said she'd go with me to the clam beds.

It was still cloudy—chilly, too. To my surprise, we saw Jim on the deserted beach, tossing his Aerobie and catching it by himself.

"I bet you were hoping we'd come by," Micale said to him.

I cringed, but Jim smiled at her. "Never can tell what you'll find on the beach," he said.

"Is that the latest in Boy Scout jewelry?" she asked him.

He touched the red and yellow braided plastic necklace around his neck. He had a matching ring on his finger. "Yeah," he said. "A friend made it for me."

"Male or female?" Micale wanted to know.

He bugged his eyes at her. "Micale, did anyone ever tell you you're nosy?"

"Sure. Nosy and pushy, that's me," she said.

"So what're you doing about it?"

"Nothing. I like me the way I am."

"How's your float for the parade coming?" I asked him to keep them from fighting with each other.

"It's ready," Jim said. "The guys made this neat tepee, and we got some real trees from the nursery and a plastic reindeer that doesn't look too fake. How's your clown act coming?"

"Act?" I said. "We're just going to wear costumes and walk behind your truck."

"Clowns are supposed to be funny," he said, echoing Micale. "You could wear big shoes and trip each other up. Do you know how to do pratfalls?"

"No." I pressed my lips together, trying to hide my panic.

"You could pretend to drop stuff in each other's pants. Like a firecracker," Jim suggested. "I saw a clown do that in a circus. When it exploded, he jumped up and went running around with his pants on fire. It was hysterical."

"Hysterical!" I squawked. "No way. Not me."

Micale's eyes were flashing like a video game. "I've got it," she said. "How about you go around being poker-faced and scolding me, Meg, and I creep around behind you doing tricks."

"No tricks!" I squeaked.

"What kind of tricks?" Jim asked her.

"It doesn't matter. What's funny is me trying to do them and Meg catching me and shaking her finger in my face. Like I could try to give her a hotfoot or make her slip on a banana peel."

"And it'll be hilarious to see me break my neck," I said. "You can laugh all the way to the emergency room." Because that's what would happen, I knew.

"But, Meg, I wouldn't actually be doing anything to you," Micale said, as if I were totally unreasonable.

"What about an unraveling sweater?" Jim said. "One of you could wear something that keeps unraveling, and the other one could be rolling up the wool."

Suddenly, they'd become a team to force me into doing a comedy act. I lost control. "I'm not funny," I shouted. "I've never been funny. I don't want to be funny. I *hate* having people laugh at me."

They both stood there staring at me. Then they began laughing. I couldn't believe it. I'd lost my temper and they thought I was funny! "Ohhh, this is awful!" I wailed.

Micale laughed harder. "Catch," Jim said as he winged his Aerobie at me. I jumped and caught it. "Awesome," he said.

For the next few minutes we whipped the Aerobie around among the three of us, and I leapt and stretched, showing off for him. When he leapt, his belly button showed like a plump, round raisin. He's so beautiful. I loved watching him. I loved playing with him. The parade disappeared from my mind. I was having a great time.

All of a sudden I realized I was supposed to be doing the clam beds. If I didn't get to it soon, the tide would turn. "I have to go," I said and picked up my equipment.

"Aw, come on, stay, Meg," Jim said.

"Can't." I explained about the clam beds.

"Don't you know Meg's the worker. *I'm* the play-person," Micale said. "I'll stay."

"Yeah? But she's the one that can catch," he said.

His approval made me quivery. I trudged off wondering if Micale was right and he did like me. What if he did? What if he was shy, and I should be calling him up and inviting him to come over. Just because some of Micale's notions were flaky didn't mean they all were. I could pick out what to go along with and what to resist, couldn't I? It would be stupid to nix everything she suggested.

I looked out over the bay where clouds had split to show a shining island of blue. Probably what Jim wanted was a playgirl. Someone like Micale who talked easily. Boys didn't like a girl who was too se-rious. I stopped walking. What if I skipped the clam beds? I could but— No. Goofing off wasn't going to transform me. It would just make me guilty. And I hated feeling guilty.

When I got back to the cottage, Micale said Jim

had told her about a picnic after the parade for all the participants. Hot dogs and hamburgers on the beach. "And don't think I don't plan ahead, too, Meg. I asked Jim if we could get a ride home with him, and he said he thought so. So *now* are you glad you're going to be a clown?" She was smiling at me as if she already knew my answer.

"I'd rather be an Indian maiden or the Statue of Liberty," I said.

"Jim'll like you better as a clown. Trust me," Micale said. "It'll show you're a good sport, not just a pretty face."

Trust her. My intuition said, "Don't," but he *had* seemed enthused about the idea of us being clowns. I could do it. And maybe it'd be good for me—sort of like bad-tasting medicine was good for you. I'd make myself do it. Being a clown for one morning couldn't be that awful. I hoped.

CHAPTER

ELEVEN

MICALE

Meg was in a black mood. I'd come right out and asked her what was eating her, but she wouldn't say. I figured it had to be either her mother or me. Well, Heather was due home from work to dress up for mussel stew night at George's. She called from the sandwich shop, where she was working with the part-timer George had hired, to ask us if we wanted her to pick up something for our supper.

"Don't bother getting us anything. I'll make spaghetti," Meg told her, and she asked me, "You'll eat *that*, won't you?"

"Sure," I said. "So long as you don't put onions in it. I hate onions."

Meg rolled her eyes and told Heather that spaghetti would suit me fine.

"Boy, you make it sound like I'm hard to please or something," I complained, after she hung up and came back to where I was sitting cross-legged on the living room floor with the sewing kit. She just grunted. I was trying to pin the valentine shorts on her so they wouldn't slide off her narrow hips. "Stop twitching," I said. "I almost jabbed the pin in your butt that time."

"Do we have to do this now, Micale?" Meg said.

"Just hold still for two minutes and I'll be done." She was probably fidgety about Heather. I'd heard her quizzing Heather this morning about who was going to be at George's house besides her. "Nobody" was the answer, and Meg hadn't liked that.

"You know," I said, "I still think we could walk by George's house tonight and just check out how she's doing."

"No," Meg said. "I will not sneak around spying on my mother. And you better not either."

"Okay, okay." I could imagine poor old George knocking himself out on his day off, cooking up a gourmet dinner and cleaning up his house for company. "They'll probably just eat and talk and neck a little anyway. This is only their first real date, after all."

"Micale, please, I *don't* want to discuss it with you."

"Touchy," I said. "You're so touchy." The shorts were pinned. I began sewing them up the back. I hadn't done a thing to make her hate me, but lately Meg was talking to me like I was an especially obnoxious green crab. I opened my mouth to have it out with her, but just then Heather blew in.

"Have you guys eaten dinner yet?"

"Haven't even started it, Mom," Meg said.

"You look cute in those shorts." Heather smiled. Then the smile sagged a little. "Well, you can save me some of the spaghetti. There's been a change of plans. George called to say someone dropped in on him unexpectedly and could we do the dinner Sunday night instead."

"Oh, Mom, I'm sorry," Meg said.

"Actually," Heather said, "it's just as well. I broke a tooth on, would you believe it, a sour ball? But the boy George hired told me about a dentist in Orleans who's got evening office hours. So I'm going down there, and his nurse said she'll try to squeeze me in, but she doesn't know when. You want to bet I'll be sitting there waiting all evening?"

"Does the tooth hurt?" I asked.

"No, but missing dinner with George does." Heather grabbed a book for the long haul in the dentist's office and buzzed off.

Meg was looking thoughtful. She always looks thoughtful, but this was intense. I clamped my lips shut to keep from saying what I was thinking because she obviously didn't want to discuss her mother's love life with me. But then Meg said, "He breaks his date with Mom just because someone drops in. Huh! I wonder what kind of someone that is."

Just what I'd been wondering. I said, "Let's find out."

"You mean spy on his house?"

"Your mother won't be there. We can just sort of casually peek in the windows to see who's there. Or is that against your principles, too?"

"I don't know."

"Come on, Meg. If you're walking down a street at night and the drapes aren't drawn, you look in, don't you?"

"I guess we could look. I mean—"

"It's important to find out if he's got another woman in his life."

She brooded for a few minutes, then said, "I'll make the spaghetti." First, she went in our room to take off the shorts. I left her alone. She'd come around. She wanted to find out who George was entertaining more than I did. I picked up the horror story I was reading and finished the chapter.

"I'll do the dishes," I said after we ate the spaghetti.

Meg took our two plates and forks to the sink and started washing them as if she hadn't heard me. "If we're going to spy on George, we ought to wait until it gets dark," she said, "which means leaving here around eight. Are you scared of the dark?"

"Who, me? I'm not scared of anything—except things that bite." Anyway, why should I be scared when I had as my partner—Meg, captain of the basketball team, the cool commander. She looked as if she could take on a werewolf if we met one.

"Wear something dark," she told me, "so we

won't be too visible." She had on her jeans and long-sleeved blue shirt.

"Got ya," I said happily. Our evening was shaping up to be exciting. Then a wicked idea hit me. Meg needed me on this expedition. I couldn't see her doing it alone. "You know," I drawled, as if the idea was just dawning on me, "you did almost convince me. It really isn't very nice to spy on people."

Meg did a double take. Micale with principles? Well, actually I don't have many, but I was angling to make a bargain. "Maybe we shouldn't do this. Or you could go alone," I said slyly. "I won't tell."

Meg's brown eyes got soulful-looking. "I wish you'd go with me," she said.

"Why?"

"Because I've never done anything like this. Anyway, it was your idea."

"And you need me, right?"

She shrugged. There, I had her. "Okay, I'll go, if you'll let me design our clown costumes any way I want," I said.

She groaned. She argued. She complained, but eventually she gave in. Good. I expected her to look hilarious in the other wig I'd brought in my tote bag, the curly one from my weird scientist costume for last Halloween.

The sky was still light when we set out. Being early summer, it wouldn't get dark until close to nine o'clock. "I hope they haven't finished eating," I said. "Maybe we should have gone earlier. If they're in a bedroom or something, we won't be able to see them."

Meg gave me a dirty look.

"Well, I mean we need to catch them downstairs to see if it's a man or a woman, and if it's a woman, what she looks like. That's what we're going to see, right?"

"That better be all we see," she said.

It was a long hike down the narrow road. I tried to thumb a ride but nobody stopped. The trees stretched into big black shadows that hung over us as it got darker. It seemed to me that the lighted windows of the cottages in the woods were too far away for comfort. I needed some conversation to distract me from being scared.

"What was your father like?" I asked Meg.

"I never knew him. He left when I was born. I remember my grandfather though. I can remember him taking me into his vegetable garden and letting me pick out the ripest tomatoes. He was a sweet man. He died when I was in kindergarten."

The way she said it made me feel bad for her. I wondered what I'd remember about my father if I lost him. Sitting in his lap and reading headlines together maybe. And once when I was sick, he'd read to me in bed, and once when I'd gotten stuck in a tree, he got me down. Yeah, I probably had lots of stuff to remember about my dear old Dadsy.

We didn't go down George's long driveway this time, but circled around past somebody else's house to the top of a dune. Lots of trees were there, and we could see the back of George's house. We scrunched down behind a shaggy bush.

George's kitchen looked like a lit stage set below us. He and a bald-headed man built like George were sitting at a long table next to glass doors that opened onto the deck. The bald-headed man was doing most of the talking. George kept nodding. Then he'd reach out to pat the man on the shoulder, or he'd put some more food on his plate. It looked like the guy was telling George some long, sad story—very long. Watching them was kind of boring. George got up to go to the kitchen.

"Wake me up when the plot thickens," I said and lay back with my arms behind my head to stare at the stars.

Meg was clutching her knees and peering intently. Finally, she said, "We might as well go now. It just made me suspicious that he didn't have Mom come to dinner anyway, even if this guy showed up unexpectedly."

"I bet it's not a friend," I said. "I bet it's a relative asking for money or something, and George doesn't want Heather getting a bad impression of his family."

"He's bringing in coffee," Meg said.

I looked. George was laughing. I smacked some tough mosquitoes that the bug repellent wasn't repelling. "I think the T.V. at home would be more interesting," I said.

"Okay, let's go." Meg stood up.

"Well, aren't you relieved?"

"I don't know anything about him yet, Micale," she pointed out. "He could have all kinds of things wrong with him."

It was so dark now, we had to *feel* our way back to the road. Just as we were passing the yard of the house next to George's, a male voice said, "That's them. I told you they were girls. Let's get 'em."

Instant adrenaline. Meg and I sprinted for the road. It was lighter there. I looked over my shoulder and saw boys piling out of a tent. There were three at least and they looked big. Terror turned me into a champion sprinter. I had no trouble keeping up with Meg as we raced down Pilgrim Springs Road. What I'd do, I decided, was jump into the path of any passing car to make it stop and save us, but our luck— no cars in sight.

"Make for the first lighted house," Meg said. "We'll bang on the door until they let us in."

Now the boys came thundering so close behind us I didn't dare risk a peek. Any minute we'd be caught. Meg and I swerved into the nearest driveway. The little gray ranch house it led to showed no lights and no cars in sight. No people. No help. Bad news.

In a panic, I pounded on the front door anyway, yelling at the top of my lungs. Behind me, Meg had stopped and was facing the boys. The three of them were grinning evilly.

"You guys beat it," she said bravely.

"Grab her. I'll take the shrimp," one of the three said.

She kicked out and slammed her shoulder into the boy in front of her. Meanwhile I ducked the tall, skinny guy and ran toward the road screeching, "Billie, Mrs. Ryan, save us. Get 'em, Billie, get 'em. Good dog." I made a barking sound, and skidded and fell. A car stopped short of running over me and a man started yelling out his window at me.

"What's the matter with you? You wanna get killed?"

"Those boys are after us," I said.

"What boys?" he wanted to know.

I looked around. The boys had gone into hiding. Meg came down the driveway. She was crying quietly, and she looked sort of roughed up. "You okay?" the man asked her.

"Yes, thank you," she said stiffly. "Come on, Micale, let's go."

"Get in and I'll give you a lift," he said. He had thick eyebrows and a young face.

I put my hand on the door, but Meg yanked me away. "No thanks. We'll walk," she said quickly. The guy hesitated a minute and then took off. We started walking home.

"Why didn't you want to get a ride?" I asked her as I watched the taillights of our savior disappear.

"You'd get in a car alone with a man you don't know?"

I thought about it. "Yeah, I guess not," I said.

Then, who should we see walking toward us but a pair of familiar shapes, in fact just the ones I'd pretended to be seeing when I needed them most. "Billie! Mrs. Ryan!" I yelled.

"Is that you, Micale?" Mrs. Ryan called while her brave pooch whimpered and tried to hide behind her. Good thing Billie hadn't really been around when the boys were there. As an attack dog, she was a bust. "What are you girls doing out this late?" Mrs. Ryan asked.

"Just walking," Meg said.

"Your mother lets you walk alone at night?"

"Not really. Mom's not home."

"I'd better see you home then. You don't want to go strolling around in the dark alone, even here. I wouldn't myself if I didn't have Billie to protect me." She said it so straight-faced that I couldn't tell if she was joking.

I bent down and let the sheep-faced spaniel lick my face. "Hi, you big woolly coward, you," I said.

Mrs. Ryan chuckled. "You should see her during a thunderstorm with her hind end in the air, trying to crawl under my bed."

I started telling Mrs. Ryan about the kids who had attacked us. ". . . There were three of them and they were big guys," I said.

"No, they weren't," Meg said. "They weren't much older than us, and one of them was a skinny thing."

"But they were tough," I said. "But Meg's tougher. She beat them up."

Meg giggled. "And Micale scared them off by barking like a dog and yelling for Billie to get them." It did seem pretty funny now that it was over.

When we said good-bye to Mrs. Ryan and were safely back in the cottage, I said, "Mrs. Ryan'd make a great mother, wouldn't she?"

"You've already got a good mother," Meg said.

"Ma? Believe me, being her daughter's the pits. She expects too much."

"You might try giving her what she expects once in a while."

"Now that's not nice, Meg," I said. "You're picking on me."

She smiled. "Why not? You're always picking on me. Personally, Micale, I think you're a lucky kid." The way she said it, I figured that the adventure had done one thing for us. She was liking me a little better even though all I'd done was bark like a dog and run.

Meg went into the kitchen to make popcorn, leaving me to think. It was true that my parents made the world a pretty safe and comfortable place for me, I mean compared to how Meg had it with Heather. Heather was defenseless as a baby clam. She needed to be protected from predators, and who else was around to protect her but Meg. She was just a kid, but she was knocking herself out to be tough and shrewd as a veteran cop. Yeah, in some ways, I was lucky.

I wondered if Ma would be pleased to get a letter from me. She'd made some snide remark about not supposing that I'd ever write. Maybe I'd write her and say I was glad Grandma was feeling better and say something nice—like that I was sure Grandma must appreciate having Ma to boss her around. Yeah, something nice like that, and I'd write it in my best handwriting so that Ma couldn't complain about not being able to read it. I could even freak Dad out by writing him, too. He'd probably never had a letter from me all to himself. I could ask him how his research paper was coming and if he'd lost any weight yet. I could even tell him I missed him. Actually, the truth was I did.

TWELVE

"Amazing," Mom said when I walked into the living room in the clown outfit with my face whitened and my nose reddened and the hideous wig that made me look like a baboon. "I'd never have dreamed you'd make such a good clown, Meg."

I groaned. "I don't want to be a good clown. If I have to wear a costume, I want one that makes me look gorgeous and glamorous."

"In the Fourth of July parade?" Mom asked.

"I could be the Statue of Liberty. I could wear a sheet and a crown."

"You'd look silly," Micale said. She was perched on the arm of the couch like a vulture with her chin on her knees. "Listen, I promise you by the end of this parade, Jim's going to be so smitten, he'll even ask you for a date."

"Meg's too young for a date," Mom said.

"To go for a swim? To play a hot game of Aerobie?" Micale improvised fast.

Mom sighed. "You girls are only twelve. What's the rush?"

"I'm in no rush. It's Meg who's the practicing adult," Micale said.

The silly sunglasses with fake eyes, I thought, one of Micale's stupid joke gifts. I ran to the bedroom and put them on. At least they hid me so you couldn't tell who I was. But back in the living room, Mom and Micale talked me out of the glasses. Mom didn't like that I couldn't see too well out of them, and she and Micale swore that the wig and painted face disguised me enough. On my bottom half I wore baggy green pants hanging from red suspenders. The pants hung so low that the Valentine heart boxer shorts Micale had basted together for me showed. Below that were the floppy red sneakers that George had contributed.

I went to look at myself in Mom's full-length mirror. Yeah, I made a good clown. My heart sank. All my life I'd tried not to stand out in a crowd. What was I doing in a costume that demanded attention? That would make people laugh at me? No, I couldn't do it. "Micale," I called from Mom's bedroom. "You'll have to go by yourself. I don't feel well." I really didn't.

"You can't chicken out on me now," Micale said.

"She won't," Mom assured her. "Meg's a good sport."

"But my stomach's out of whack. And I feel faint."

"That's nerves," Micale said. "Buck up, kid. You're the fearless crab picker. You're brave."

"I am not."

"Meg, you promised Micale," Mom said.

I gritted my teeth. I'd let myself be set up to behave like a fool in public, and it was my own fault for letting Micale railroad me into it.

Mom dropped us off at the pier on her way to work an hour before the parade was supposed to start. "Don't worry," she told me. "It'll all be over soon."

I groaned. Somehow I didn't find that comforting.

"Now if for some reason you don't get a ride back with your friend Jim," Mom said, "you can hike over to the sandwich shop, and I'll run you home." She smiled at us both and looked around the pier. A fire truck was already there as well as an old-fashioned car and a truck with the Historical Society display of ladies churning butter and ironing clothes.

"This looks like such fun," Mom said. "I wish I could stay to watch. You better tell me all about it tonight. Smile, Meg."

"I'm supposed to be a sad clown," I reminded her. It was an effort to make myself let go of the car door.

"Meg, you're breaking my heart. Smile, for me, honey."

I obliged. Mom reached out through the window, hugged me and took off. Micale had gone to talk to some lady who was blowing up balloons with the kind of machine you rent.

"Meg, come here," Micale waved me over. "We can hand out balloons as we walk. Isn't that a neat idea?"

I considered, then nodded. Rather than just look silly, it would be better to be busy giving something away.

We each took enough balloons to lift us off the ground if there'd been any wind, but it was a still, sunny morning. "Now, I'm trusting you girls to hand these out one at a time to any little kids you see, say anybody under five or six," the woman instructed us.

"Don't worry," Micale said. "We won't clown around with these."

The lady laughed and we walked away with a fistful of balloons each.

More trucks with displays on them drove onto the pier and lined up behind the fire truck and the old-fashioned car. A bunch of kids I recognized from school were on a flatbed truck setting up to play steel drums. The liquid sounds tickled my ears as they tried out their instruments. "They're good," Micale said. She pulled me over to hear them practice.

"Is that you, Meg?" an eighth grader I knew from the library asked me. She was up on the truck playing a drum the size of a garbage can.

"It's me sort of," I said. I was done for. Here's

someone who barely knew me and she'd recognized me. Weakly, I asked her, "Want a balloon?"

"No thanks. It's a great costume. I'd never have recognized you," she said.

Which didn't make a lot of sense, but then neither did my being there. She kept staring at me while I squirmed, until the band leader got the drummers playing a piece together and the eighth grader had to concentrate. People who had parked on the pier to catch the start of the parade gathered around the truck to listen. I'm no expert on steel drums, but this group's rhythms made my body dissolve into separate moving parts. For a minute I was in the music and out of myself. Then I heard people laughing.

I looked and saw Micale doing a fake limbo. She staggered backward, her arms windmilling and fell. Some boy caught her. Jim! He stood her up. She clasped her hands over her heart, as if she were saying, "My hero." Then she tried to get him to dance with her, but he shook his head and backed away. His face was dabbed with war paint and he wore a headband with a feather. She pulled him into the circle that had gathered around her. The people who'd come early to watch the parade were enjoying her antics. Their laughter was all the encouragement Micale needed. She put her hands on her hips and wiggled around Jim. He stood there grinning with with his arms folded and his biceps bulging, the cutest blond Indian brave in moccasins, tan pants and a loincloth I'd ever seen. Except that he didn't look too authentic with that hair and cotton pants.

"Show her how to do the limbo, Jim," someone playing a steel drum up on the truck called out. The voice was so deep I thought it was a boy until I looked and saw a girl, small and really beautiful with big dark eyes and long dark hair.

"Go, Jimmy, go," she called as she beat out clip-clop rhythms on her drum. Around her neck was a familiar necklace. She was wearing the red and yellow woven plastic ring, too, not what a girl like her would wear unless—I turned toward Jim. He was dancing. I didn't know he had it in him to dance like that, especially alone with people watching. He was bending backward from the knees and jumping forward in time to the music. He was really good, but all I saw was the necklace and ring on him, red and yellow woven plastic just like hers.

Somebody made it for him, he'd said, but he hadn't answered when Micale asked if it was a girl or a boy. The answer was so plain now that I shriveled inside my clown costume.

People were clapping for Jim. A young couple held up a rope for him to go under. Micale got a laugh by scrunching down and crawling under it on her hands and knees. She stood up and bowed to everyone as if she'd done something wonderful, and they laughed some more.

I stood like a cardboard figure, watching them. Someone tugged at my sleeve. "Can I have a balloon?" a little boy asked me. It took me a few seconds before I could focus on what he wanted from me. "Blue," he said. I finally gave him a blue balloon.

"We're going to start," someone called through a bullhorn. "Everyone take your place." The pier was crowded now with the lineup of trucks and cars and people in the parade, as well as all the parked cars of the people there to watch it.

Micale grabbed my hand. She'd recovered her balloons from wherever she'd stowed them while she was clowning with Jim. He was climbing onto the truck with the tepee and the tree and the fake deer. So were a half a dozen other boys dressed as Indians. One fitted an arrow to a bow and pretended to shoot at the deer, which stood near the tailgate that Micale and I were supposed to follow.

I wondered if the girl in the steel drum band was the same one who'd invited Jim to the eighth-grade party.

"Listen," Micale said. "Instead of just handing out balloons, let's run back and forth from one side of the street to the other and pretend to get in each other's way as we pass, okay?"

I shook my head, but she pushed me in the direction she wanted. I stumbled toward a girl on the sidelines and handed her a balloon. Micale lurched past me as I shuffled back to the truck tailgate. "Keep going," she said. I did and gave a balloon to an old lady on the right. People laughed as if my mistake were funny. The business of handing out the balloons kept me from thinking. Every time I went back toward the tailgate, Micale would bump into me and back off and bump again trying to pass. Then she'd put her hands on her hips, pretending to get mad at me and people would laugh. Once Micale stepped on my sneaker. I would have fallen if somebody on the sidelines hadn't caught me. Everybody thought that was really humorous. Somehow, I'd become a clown in spite of myself.

A couple of streets later, Micale started grabbing my suspenders as she staggered past me.

"Stop that," I warned her. The boxer shorts weren't basted all that well. Instead of listening to me, she made it part of the act, throwing her arms up over her head and high-stepping away as if I might attack her. I was going to kill her after the parade was over. I should have done it before, I was thinking, and then it happened.

The second time we crossed paths, I tried to dodge around Micale, but instead of the suspenders, she caught the waist of my boxer shorts. They ripped open. The suspenders fell off my shoulders and there I stood in a pair of torn old white cotton underpants in front of the Boy Scouts on the truck and half the town of Wellfleet. I screamed and yanked up my baggy jeans. Micale got behind me and threw her arms around me. The crowd hooted and whistled as if it hadn't been an accident but part of the act.

I shut my eyes hoping to die. When I didn't, I shoved loose from Micale and went clumping along in those stupid oversized sneakers through the crowd and into an alley between two stores. I hung onto my jeans with one hand and the balloons with the other and kept going until a fence blocked me.

Micale was right behind me. "Meg, I didn't mean it," she said when the fence stopped me. "I really didn't."

"Get away from me," I growled.

"I'm sorry. I'm really sorry. But it wasn't on purpose. You know that. It was an accident. You know that, don't you?"

I ignored her. I pretended she didn't exist, and I asked myself out loud, "How am I going to get rid of these balloons now?"

"Just let them go," Micale said. "Forget the balloons."

"No," I said. "That's not right." I frowned at her, too numb even to hate her. Inside I was just a big empty hole. It was strange not to be feeling anything. I guess I was in shock or something. Micale began patting my arm.

"Stop it," I said, shuddering at her touch. "Go away and leave me alone."

"Don't be mad at me, Meg," she begged. "I'll do anything you say. I'll swim across the bay and let the crabs eat me—anything."

Think, a voice inside me commanded. It was like I was suddenly two people, one that was helpless as a puppet and the other this voice. *You can't stand there with your back against the fence holding a fistful of balloons forever,* the voice said. I came to on a flood of feelings. I wanted to rip off the clown costume, but I couldn't unless I was willing to walk home in my disgusting torn underpants. I wanted to tromp over to the sandwich shop and throw myself into my mother's arms, but the parade was in my way.

The horns of a brass band blared somewhere nearby. I hadn't noticed that brass band in the parade. They probably hadn't spotted me either. Suddenly I felt calm. After what Jim had seen, I could never meet his eyes again. Never. Besides, he had a girlfriend, which meant he hadn't liked me in the first place. Micale had misled me about that, too.

"Please," Micale begged. "Say something. You can hit me if it'll help."

"I have to hand out the rest of these balloons," I said. I hauled up my jeans and knotted the suspenders together. Then I pushed past Micale and went back down the alley, getting to the main street in time to fall in behind the truck that carried the brass band. Micale followed me.

"I can't believe you," she yelled in my ear. "You're amazing."

I paid no attention to her. I wasn't amazing. I just needed to get rid of the balloons and get home where I could hole up and lick my wounds.

I handed a balloon to a mother with a baby, and

another to the little boy standing next to her. He smiled at me but hid behind his mother so that just the red balloon stuck out. Nobody was snickering and pointing his finger at me. Probably nobody watching the parade here had seen what happened. I kept doling out balloons, giving one to every kid I spotted, but without the slapstick stuff. Micale was doing her Groucho Marx walk and leaving me alone.

By the end of the parade route, I was worn out and my feet were sore and blistered.

"You girls going to the picnic?" a man in an old-fashioned car decorated with red, white and blue streamers asked us. "Climb aboard if you want a ride."

Micale looked at me. "We going?"

"Not me," I said.

"Why not? Jim won't tease you. For all you know he didn't even see."

"He saw."

"But you don't know how he's going to act. It might be all right, Meg."

"I'm going home. You do what you want."

"Well, if you're going home, I'll go with you," Micale said. The man who had offered us a ride left.

Micale stuck her thumb out. A car with a family in it stopped for us. "Where you going?" the woman asked us. When Micale told her, the woman said they'd drop us off at the supermarket on the corner of Cove Road and Route 6.

"Thanks," Micale said and hopped in the front.

Since the two little kids in the back made hitching a ride seem reasonably safe, I got in with them.

"You were in the parade?" asked the woman, who was sitting between her husband and Micale.

"Yeah, it was fun," Micale said.

The woman said they were renting for a couple of weeks and asked if we were local girls. Micale told her that we were staying at Aunt Jane's house for the summer. She and the woman agreed that the Wellfleet Fourth of July parade was a fine tradition, so basic American, so good for children. Micale shot me a guilty look over her shoulder. I stared out the window.

We walked home barefooted from Route 6 after they dropped us off. Micale's feet were blistered, too.

"See," Micale said. "That lady didn't know what happened to you. I bet hardly anybody saw it. It happened so fast."

"Jim saw it."

"Really, I'm really, really sorry," Micale said two or three times. "And Meg, that was so gutsy of you to get back in that parade. I couldn't have done it. You're really strong. I really admire you so much."

"Micale, shut up. Really."

"Well, okay, but what I want to tell you is, I think if you just act with Jim like you did—I mean, just act like it never happened, he won't say anything. I mean, probably he's just as embarrassed as you are."

I put my hands over my ears. I couldn't stop her from talking, but I wasn't about to listen. I thought about the dim cave of my room where I could hide and sleep out my miseries. First though, I ought to take Micale's tote bag, stuff it with all her junk, including every silly gift she'd given me, and toss it out the window. I ought to, but probably I wouldn't. I've always known something terrible would happen if I ever lost control, especially with Micale. I had an urge to kill her. How could I have let her force me to be a clown?

THIRTEEN

MICALE

All of a sudden I didn't exist. I mean, I left Meg alone like she wanted because I figured one good night's sleep and she'd realize it could have been worse. Like what if she hadn't worn anything under the boxer shorts? But sleeping didn't do a thing for her.

Saturday I woke up late and nobody was in the house. Not even a note. Well, I knew Heather had gone off to work, but where was Meg? When I came out of the bathroom, I listened to the refrigerator humming inside and the wind blowing outside, and both sounded unfriendly. I wasn't welcome in that cottage anymore. It was eerie. It didn't buck me up any either to recall Heather's reaction after I told her what had happened to Meg in the parade. She kept saying, "Oh, Micale. Oh, Micale," and then she went off to comfort Meg, and I didn't see either of them for hours.

The thing to do was find Meg and have it out with her. I chased all the way down the beach to the clam flats against a wind strong enough to lean on, but no Meg. Maybe she was hiding out on me. I didn't blame her after what I'd done to her. But she couldn't stay mad at me forever, could she? I finally settled down in the living room to read a book of Japanese folktales from Aunt Jane's collection. A while later Meg drifted in. "Hi," I said. "What's up?"

"Nothing." She wouldn't look at me, just went into her room and closed the door. Being ignored is the one punishment I can't stand. I followed her into the bedroom. She was lying on her bed looking out the window.

"Hey," I said, "yell at me or something. Tell me you hate me. I know you do. You can even throw something at me. I won't duck."

She shook her head with a look sad enough to bring me to my knees, but I stayed on the attack for another round. "Well, how long are you going to be depressed?" I asked, as if it were all her fault.

"I don't know."

"All right then. Let's go for a walk and talk it over."

"I'm tired, Micale."

She was so polite. How could I win against politeness that thick? "So what are you doing this afternoon then?" I was still pretending we were connecting.

"I don't know." She wouldn't look at me.

I apologized all over again to the back of her head. I explained how I hadn't meant to embarrass her. "You can't hold an accident against me forever, Meg," I said. But she didn't turn around. Nothing. Not a word. Finally I gave up and left her alone. What else could I do? She had excluded me from her universe. I was banished to outer space. I went for a walk by myself to think it over.

If Meg kept treating me like a nonperson, I might as well leave Wellfleet. What I'd do was call Ma, admit I'd flunked out here and say I wanted to join her or Dad, whichever one was willing to reclaim their rejected only child. Boy, did I hate that idea!

Give it another day or two, I told myself. Don't rush into defeat. Make it come get you. Meanwhile, since I was on the road to Jim Bruder's house, I decided to get his opinion on how to deal with Meg.

Nobody answered when I knocked on his front door. I walked around to the back and found Jim tying up tomato plants in a vegetable garden. "Hey, how's it going?" I said.

He looked over his shoulder and didn't seem surprised to find me trespassing. "Okay, Micale. How about you?"

"I'm in purgatory. Meg's not talking to me."

"You and she have a fight?"

"Not exactly," I said.

"Too bad you didn't go to the picnic after the parade. It was fun."

"Well, Meg was too embarrassed about what happened to her."

"Yeah. I can see that . . . You didn't do it on purpose, did you?"

"I absolutely did *not*."

"So what did you two fight about?"

"We didn't fight. I wish we had. She's just not talking."

"Oh." He turned toward me, still on one knee, and scratched his nose. "It happened so fast. When she lost her pants. Nobody much noticed except me and a couple of the other scouts, and they don't know her well enough to tease her. Anyway, she wasn't standing there bare butt or anything. Tell her she can forget it."

"You tell her. Please!"

"Me? *I'm* not going to talk to her about it. You crazy?"

"Do you like Meg?" I asked flat out.

He looked puzzled. "Sure. She's a nice kid."

I had one of my brilliant ideas. "Jim, the square dancing begins next Wednesday, right? I bet if you called and asked Meg to go, she'd cheer up."

"Well, but I'm meeting my girlfriend at the square dance." He pointed to the plastic braid around his neck.

My jaw dropped. Uh-oh. I wondered if Meg knew. That'd give her something else to be depressed about. I might as well call out my parental rescue squad now. Things were worse than I'd thought.

"Listen," he said. "Tell Meg to pretend like nothing happened. That's the best way." He had a really cute smile. Yeah, I could see what Meg liked about him.

That night after supper, Heather said she was in the mood for ice cream. "I'll go to the store with you," I offered when she asked who was coming with her. The instant I said I'd go, Meg said she couldn't. Too busy reading letters she'd gotten from her friends in Saratoga, she claimed.

The pickup was barely out of earshot of the house when I burst out with, "Your daughter hates me, and I don't know how to make her stop."

Heather squinted at me. "What Meg hates is looking foolish. You didn't mean to do it, did you, Micale?"

"It was an accident," I wailed.

"Well, let her be for a while; she'll eventually get over it."

"Eventually? How long's that? By 'eventually' I'll die of neglect."

Heather laughed as if I were joking. "Give her a week," she said. "Meg's too fair to stay mad at you when you didn't hurt her on purpose."

"Unless she won't believe I didn't do it on purpose. What then?"

"Just give her time. Meg's too sensible to brood for very long."

Heather knew her daughter better than I did. All right then, I'd try to survive another day or two in the frost zone.

"Actually, I'd like Meg to be recovered by tomorrow," Heather said. "George is coming for dinner. I've invited him here to give Meg a chance to get to know him. You'll help me entertain him, won't you, Micale?"

"Sure." I was glad to be wanted for something.

Ma called in the morning. She said she and Grandma got a big laugh out of my express mail letter and that I seemed to be maturing.

"Ma," I confessed, "I'm really not doing too well here. Meg's not talking to me. If she doesn't start soon, could I come hang out with you and the grandma for a while?"

"What did you do to her?" Ma asked, instantly sure that it had to be my fault that Meg wasn't talking to me.

I gave her a brief rundown on the parade. My mother gasped. "Micale, how could you?"

For the umpteenth time I used the word *accident*.

"Did you tell her you were sorry?" Ma asked as if I were too much of an idiot to think of that by myself, and she rushed on to insult me some more. "You know, Micale, pulling down Meg's pants in public may have seemed funny to you, but to her—"

"Ma!" I yelled. "I did not do it on purpose, and I apologized about a million times. I'm not an emotional retard. I know how bad she felt."

"Don't raise your voice to me, Micale," Ma said.

So we were right back to our usual hackles-raised standoff, but then my mother said, "Your grandmother was saying she'd like to see you."

"Really? Grandma wants to see me?"

"Actually, I miss you, too."

"You do? You really miss me, Ma?"

"Occasionally—in my weaker moments."

I ignored the qualifier and said, "I miss *you*, Ma."

Dead silence. I guess heavy stuff like that coming from me threw her.

"Well, think about it. Meanwhile, I'll get a bus schedule," Ma told me. "Then if you want to come to Ohio, you can. But I'm warning you, it's muggy and there isn't anything for you to do here."

Heather said we weren't going to fuss for George, but it looked to me like she was fussing when she started cutting up beef into little squares and skewering them with onions and tomatoes and green pepper pieces.

"Can I help?" I asked. It had rained all day Sunday, and I'd gotten tired of watching Meg clean the house. Her mother was paying her this time, but still, I felt bad lifting my feet so she could vacuum under them while I sat there reading.

"You can cut up a salad if you want," Heather said. "I think I'll cook the potatoes and mash them instead of baking them on the grill with the kabobs."

"You're going to cook outside in the rain?" I asked.

"I'm hoping it'll stop. If not, maybe I can get the barbecue under the overhang so the rain doesn't put the fire out."

Obviously, Heather was an optimist like me.

"What's for dessert?" I asked while I was cutting up salad.

"I made a chocolate mousse," Heather said.

"Yum. You really like this guy, don't you?"

Heather smiled. "George deserves to be fussed over. He's such a sweetie pie. I think some of his regular customers buy sandwiches just so they can tell him their troubles." She told me about an old man with an ailing dog and a lady whose mother-in-law had moved in.

"Does he listen to your problems?" I asked.

"Well, I tell him about Meg." Heather lowered her voice. "I don't think it's just the parade. I think it's the whole past year; she's had so many disappointments. Leaving Saratoga was hard on her—her basketball team and all the girls she's grown up with—well, you know."

I did. And if Meg knew about Jim Bruder's having a girlfriend, that was another downer. Not to mention getting stuck with me for the summer.

I finished the salad and set the table. Heather was thanking me enthusiastically when Meg came in and asked, "Do you want the bathroom cleaned, too, Mom?"

"Oh, would you, darling? Thanks."

I skulked back to my reading. There was no way I could compete in good-girledness with Meg. I'd been around for a week and a half, and she was liking me less than when I first arrived. Why was I kidding myself? She didn't just not like me, she despised me. I'd tell Ma tomorrow I was coming. She'd said she missed me. Besides, being my mother she had to put up with me, like it or not.

Both Heather and Meg got dressed up for George. Heather put on a candy-striped shirt and white pants. With her light brown hair fluffed up, and her eyes sparkling, she looked like a teenager. Meg wore a red sweater I hadn't seen before. "You look nice," I told her. "How come you're dressing up for George? I thought you didn't like him."

"I'm dressing up to please Mom. And I never said I didn't like George. I don't know him, so how can I not like him?"

"Right," I said.

Heather came in from lighting her barbecue grill. "The rain's stopped," she announced happily. "The sky's so clear you'd never know it ever rained." She looked at Meg and said, "You look lovely, darling." Then she looked at me and raised her eyebrows. "Is that the only T-shirt and pants you brought with you, Micale?"

"The jeans are clean," I said.

"But for company? Isn't there anything else in that big suitcase you could wear?"

This was the first nagging Heather had done since I arrived. Besides, I figured I owed her one for taking me in. So I dug out a flowered skirt from the over-stuffed suitcase and a shirt with a dinosaur on it that I'd stolen from a kid at a soccer game. Well, he'd given me a kick in the shins on purpose. I even brushed my hair.

"Ta-dah!" I said, back in the living room. "Here I

am, dressed up for the party." Meg looked up from her book. I could see by her expression she didn't think much of my getup.

There was a short pause while Heather put down a dip and some chips on the coffee table. Then she said, "Thank you, Micale. You look better."

At least I hadn't scored a total zero.

George had a big head and a pumpkin-size smile. He was so broad that he seemed to fill the living room as he thrust a bottle of wine and a box of candy at Heather. "What a treat," he said, "to eat dinner with three lovely ladies." Next he complimented the cottage. Heather said it was her aunt's. So George said that her aunt would certainly be pleased at the way she was keeping it. Heather said Meg was the housekeeper.

"Ah, yes, Meg, the perfect daughter," George said. He turned his grin on Meg who was watching him quietly. "Your mother claims you have no faults," he told her.

"You've told me that," she said.

His face got red. "Using the same line twice on a pretty girl—I guess I'm getting old. Forgive me. Anyway, you must. Being unforgiving is a fault."

Meg kind of blinked. Then she looked at me. I don't know what she was thinking but I smiled hopefully. There was a pause. Then Heather said, "Meg's only fault is that she worries too much. What do you want to drink, George?"

He said he'd like some wine. While they were out in the kitchen opening the bottle he'd brought, I said to Meg, "I wish my mother thought I was perfect, or even just okay. She thinks I'm a holy terror."

"You are," Meg said.

I was thrilled. She hadn't insulted me in so long I'd lost hope. Could it be that she was beginning to soften?

"Come out on the patio, girls," Heather called. "It's a beautiful evening." Meg picked up the chips and dip and we went.

"So, what do you think of Wellfleet?" George asked Meg.

"I love being near the beach," she said.

"And you?" he asked me.

"Well, except for the crabs and mosquitoes, it's not so bad," I said. "And the bluefish. Nothing with teeth that big should be allowed where people swim."

"Bluefish are good to eat," George said. He started describing ways to cook them in such boring detail that you knew he really loved food.

The dinner was a big success. When Meg got up to do the dishes, I went to the kitchen to help her. "He sure is cheerful," I said. "He hasn't stopped smiling. Do you like him so far?"

"So far," Meg said.

"Maybe he'll turn out to be the right one for Heather."

Meg didn't bother commenting. I tried talking

about the weather, but the freeze was still in effect. When we finished with the dishes, we went back out to the patio.

Suddenly George turned to Meg and said, "I heard you had an embarrassing experience at the parade."

"Who told you?" Meg asked anxiously.

I held my breath. Adults are supposed to be more tactful.

"I don't know," George said. "Your mother maybe."

"It wasn't Jim Bruder?" Meg asked.

"No. I haven't seen Jim this week. But why I bring it up is—I once had an embarrassment very much like yours."

"You did?" Meg was standing straight as a post with her arms folded.

"I did," he assured her, leaning back to relax. "I was maybe fifteen, and I asked this girl I liked very much for a date. 'Yes,' says she to my surprise. Good. Now, where to take her? I had no money, but it was summer and we could swim free at the community pool. Only I had no swim-suit. So I ask my big brother to lend me his. But I'm skinnier than him—then I was. So, we get to the pool, this girl and me, and I dive in to show her what a daring fellow I am, and oh-my-god—there goes the suit. Can you imagine? I quick pull it back on, but the girl says, 'I want to go home.' And the ribbing I got from my friends!"

"Nobody's teased Meg," I said.

"I've been in hiding," she said. "Nobody's seen me."

"You don't like being teased?" George said to her.

"Not very much," she said.

"If you have brothers, you get used to it," he said. "Doesn't Micale tease you?"

"I wouldn't dare," I said.

"You know what my most embarrassing moment was?" Heather put in, and she told about how she'd wet her pants in kindergarten. ". . . And when the teacher asked me, didn't I have a bathroom at home, I was so embarrassed that—would you believe?—I shook my head and said no."

I figured it was my turn. "I'm pretty hard to embarrass," I said. "But when I started clarinet lessons, my teacher said I was a fast learner. Well, I figured I was a pro. So my aunts had this party for my parents' twenty-fifth anniversary, and I volunteered to play a solo. There I stood in front of this room full of relatives and I played. It was awful. I'd only had three lessons. Even I knew it was bad. But they clapped for me when it was over. Except my mother looked as if she had a bellyache and my father kept his head down as if he wanted to hide."

When we were getting ready for bed, I tested Meg. "I've been thinking maybe I'll go see how my grandmother's making out," I said. "My mother says she's missing me."

Meg had her back to me so I couldn't see what she

was thinking, and she didn't say a word. I got under the covers, still waiting for a reaction. Nothing. She turned out the light. Well then, I'd been wrong about her insults. She hadn't let up on hating me after all. I felt really bad about it. I'd gotten kind of fond of Meg Waters.

FOURTEEN

"So it's all set," Micale came in to say while I was getting dressed Monday morning. She'd called her mother first and then Mom, who was at work. "Heather can get time off to take me to the bus stop tomorrow. She says she's sorry I'm leaving. I told her *you're* not going to be. I told her *you* can't wait to get rid of me."

"Ummm," I said.

"Admit it, Meg. Get it off your chest. It'll make you feel better."

It made me so angry that Micale was still trying to tell me what to do that I burst out with, "What do you know about how I feel?" Then I pressed my lips together to keep from fighting with her.

"Saying what you think's healthy. It's bad to keep everything in," Micale said.

"No, it isn't. What you don't say can't hurt anybody."

"Yeah, it does," she insisted. "It hurts *you*."

She was such a know-it-all that I was tempted. "You really want to know what I think of you?"

"Yeah, go ahead. Sock it to me." She prepared for my attack by sitting on the bed with her legs crossed under her and her back very straight.

"Okay." I let go at her. "I don't like you, Micale. I don't like you because you're always trying to push me around and make me do things I don't want to do. Like right now. I don't want to say mean things to you. I just want you out of my life so I can forget you." My voice had started off low and shaky, but it got louder and louder.

Micale's eyes widened and she squeaked indignantly, "What do you mean I push you around? What are you talking about?"

"What I'm talking about is—" I took a deep breath to try to rein in my temper, but it was too late. "Like that parade—"

"Now hold it," she interrupted me. "The pants thing really was an accident, Meg. It really was."

"But you made me be a clown in that parade when I didn't want to be." As soon as I said it, I realized it was unfair to put the whole blame on her. I'd let her talk me into being a clown because I wanted to be near Jim Bruder. She hadn't *made* me do it.

"I meant well," Micale said. "I sort of tricked you into it because I told you it was Jim's idea, when really it was mine, but I meant well. I really did, Meg."

It didn't surprise me at all that she'd tricked me. It was what I expected of her. I clenched my fists and asked her, "You want to hear what else I don't like about you?"

"Shoot," she said.

"You lied to me about Jim. You made me believe he liked me just so that I'd make a fool of myself."

"No, honest." Micale put her hand over her heart and held up her right hand as if she was swearing to the truth of what she said. "I thought he did like you."

I shook my head. "You used him as bait so I'd do what you wanted." The stupid tears that always showed up to shame me filled my eyes. My voice went up too high. I said, "And I'll tell you what else gets my goat. When you sit around while I do all the work like I'm your servant or something."

"I help sometimes. I helped with the dinner for George, didn't I?"

"Oh, big deal. One night you helped a little. But you could do more."

"Well, you're right. I mean when you're right, you're right. But I'm leaving. So what can I do?"

"Nothing," I said. The tears were rolling down my cheeks now, and I didn't feel better. I felt terrible.

"Anything else?" Micale asked.

Hadn't I told her enough? I tried to think of something really rotten she'd done that would make her understand why I didn't want anything to do with her, but I was too upset to think.

"I still have one last present in the tote bag to give you, but you probably wouldn't like it," Micale said.

"Presents!" I yelled, losing control again. "What kind of a present is a practical joke? I hate practical jokes. I've always hated them. And you knew that. You did, didn't you?"

She shrugged. "I was trying to loosen you up. You don't know how to be a kid, Meg. You're such an old lady. You're older than your mother."

"And you're a spoiled brat." I gasped. I'd never said anything that mean to anyone in my life.

"Well," Micale said, "so that about sums up how we feel about each other, huh? Anyway, do you want the last gift or not?"

I was furious. How could she think I'd care about whatever silly gift she had left for me? I'd never ask her what it was, never. "And I don't like the way you dress either," I snapped. "But that's your business . . . But if you wear the same clothes every day, you could wash them more often at least."

"Okay," she agreed.

"Okay, what?" I was screaming, and she was still talking in this calm, reasonable voice as if we were having a conversation instead of a fight. It was maddening.

"Okay, from now on, I'll change my clothes and wash them more, try to be more helpful, and not play practical jokes. And I won't make you do things you don't want to do. Although, it seems to me that just trying to talk somebody into something isn't the same thing as pushing them around. I mean, you could say no, couldn't you?"

What had I done? Confused, I asked her, "Now you're *not* leaving?"

"Don't worry. I'll go," she said. ". . . Unless you want me to stay?"

"Eeeeeow!" I howled insanely. Micale was impossible. Here I'd slapped her down with all my strength, and she was bouncing right back up at me like some kind of rubber monster. I had to get away from her. "I'm going to check the clam beds," I said.

"Oh, is it low tide? Well," Micale said, "I'm dog-sitting for Mrs. Ryan today. Soon as she drops Billie off, I'll meet you there."

I gaped in disbelief. After what I'd just said to her, how could any normal girl want to keep me company? It was unreal. She was unreal. I collected my gear and took off. The dune grasses were flattened against the sand because the wind was so bad, but I was glad to be outdoors where things made sense. Micale didn't. It was true she didn't understand me, but then I didn't understand her either.

The strangest thing was I'd always been afraid if I told somebody off, really let my temper loose, the world would fall to pieces, but I hit out at Micale with everything I had and she was still together. In fact, she said she was going to change. Not that she really would, but I did feel better, sort of cleaned out. She'd been right about that. Even remembering I'd exposed my torn underpants to the whole of

Wellfleet didn't make me shudder anymore. If Mom and George and Micale could get over their embarrassing moments, I'd survive mine—probably—especially if I never had to face Jim Bruder again. Or supposing I did bump into him, if he didn't say anything to me about it. Like if he just nodded and said, "Hi, Meg," I could nod back and say "hi" without dying on the spot. And if he made a remark? I could survive that, too, probably. After living with Micale, I could probably survive anything.

I was almost to the clam beds when I realized I wasn't being fair to Micale. It wasn't her fault Jim Bruder had another girlfriend. I could see how his friendliness might have fooled her into thinking he liked me. I was the one who knew him and should have realized that he's that nice to everybody. So that one I'd done to myself.

Anyway, she'd leave tomorrow and my life would go back to normal. I'd swim and do the clam beds and read and sunset watch and not take any chances. No more spying on George either. Micale was right about Mom. I can't really protect her. I'm not a better judge of men than Mom is. We both make mistakes. And she's the adult.

Above me, giant gray storm clouds were tumbling over each other. Every so often one opened up, and splat came a gust of rain. The bay was pinched up in tight little whitecaps, the kind of dramatic weather I love best. So relax and enjoy it, I told myself.

It was dead low tide on the clam flats. They

stretched out like fresh cement most of the way to Lieutenant's Island. Seed boxes were anchored in place here and there. The people who had the claims on either side of Aunt Jane's were bent over working. But as soon as I passed the yellow buoy marking the boundary of Aunt Jane's claim, I saw trouble. The rough water from the high winds must have flushed the sand out of the frames, and whatever seed clams hadn't been scattered and lost were lying exposed. A horde of green crabs was feeding on them.

I got to work picking up crabs and raking sand back over the clams. Sometimes the wind whipped my hair around my face so I couldn't see, but I kept going by feel, wishing I'd brought a barrette or a piece of string. I filled one bag, straightened up and moved to another area. A boat had been torn loose from its mooring and was lying stranded in the middle of the flats. If the owner didn't come after it, it'd float off on the next tide. I hoped the seed clams weren't going to be swept away, too. With the storm and the crabs and the days when we didn't get to the beds, it would be a miracle if Aunt Jane had anything to harvest in a couple of years. I hoped she wouldn't blame us and think we hadn't tried.

The gray clouds were swirled through with marshmallow streaks now. They were still churning, but the sky was brightening. Water was trickling back. The tide was turning. I looked around frantically. It was hopeless. I couldn't manage this by myself.

"Meg! Hey, Meg!" Micale called. She was running toward me with Billie galloping alongside her. For once Billie acted glad to see me and bounced over to lick my cheek. I put my arms around the silly beast and comforted myself by hugging her.

"Yuck. Look at those gross crabs!" Micale said. "Here, give me a bag."

Next time I looked up, Billie was lying down on the dry sand near the dune watching us from between her paws, and Micale was bent over another wooden frame picking up crabs—picking them up with her bare hands! "Micale," I called in disbelief. "What are you doing?"

"Helping you," she said.

Awesome! Micale picking crabs? I went back to work. A while later I saw Billie sleeping like a brown wool mat against the dune, and Micale was still bent over working. She looked like a little boy in her jeans and railroad cap and an old gray sweatshirt of Aunt Jane's that had hung on the back of the front door. I got teary eyed again for no reason watching her. Finally, when the water reached my ankles, I told Micale that we had to stop. We dragged the bags up to the dunes and tied them shut. Then we flopped down near Billie. She promptly came to sprawl across us, with her rear end on me and her head on Micale's arm.

"You should have seen silly Billie on the way here," Micale said. "She found a toad on the road, and sniffed at it like she'd never seen one before. So the toad hops, and Billie jumps five feet straight up—

I'm not kidding. And she hides behind me—from a toad. Can you believe it?"

"She's a clown. You're a clown, Billie, aren't you?" I tussled with the dog and threw a stone for her to chase.

"Mrs. Ryan won't be back from Boston until after dinner," Micale said. "She said if you didn't want Billie in your aunt's cottage, to put her back in her own in a couple of hours. Just so long as Billie doesn't get lonely spending the whole day by herself."

"It's funny to think of a dog getting lonely," I said.

"Well, they do," Micale said. "I know one that cried so much when he got left home alone that the neighbors made his owners get rid of him. He was a schnauzer. Cute dog . . . You never get lonely, do you, Meg?"

"Sometimes."

"Yeah. But you keep yourself busy. Like after I'm gone, you'll be too busy to think about me, right?"

"I'll think about you," I said.

"Yeah, but you won't *miss* me."

I shrugged.

"You won't . . . Well, what do you want to do with these bags of crabs?"

"I'll call Mom. She can get them with the pickup on her way home and take them to the dump or something . . . Thanks for helping, Micale. I couldn't believe it when I saw you picking up those crabs."

"Told you I was going to help, didn't I? Anyway, they're not so awful. I didn't get nipped once."

I smiled. "Too bad. If you weren't leaving, now that you're used to them, you could go swimming."

"Not with the bluefish still out there. Not me."

"There wasn't much for you to do here, I guess," I said.

"Oh, I don't know. It wasn't boring. Well, I kept things hopping, didn't I?" She grinned.

I nodded and asked, "So what'll you do in Ohio?"

"Behave myself," Micale said cheerfully, "if I know what's good for me. My mom's a lot like you. She goes according to the book and she doesn't appreciate practical jokes."

"But it'll be pretty hot in Ohio, won't it?"

"Muggy, yeah, but the grandma has air-conditioning."

"Right, and you're a city person, not a beach person."

"Well, but with nobody my age around, it won't be that much fun. Of course, I can always fight with Ma if I get too bored."

We sat there in silence for a while. I was feeling funny, as if now that she was leaving, I didn't have to hate her. Or maybe it was because she'd helped with the crabs. Or maybe I'd just used up all my emotions yelling at her. Anyway, I gave in and asked, "So what was the last practical joke? . . . From the tote bag."

"Oh. A third eye. You wear it stuck to your forehead."

I snorted and shook my head.

"Want it?" Micale asked me.

"No thanks."

"Yeah, well . . . So you'd better say good-bye to Jim for me. Tell him I had fun shooting the Aerobie around."

"No," I said. "I'm not going to see him."

"He won't give you a hard time, Meg."

"Maybe not, but there's no point in me chasing him. He has a girlfriend, a beautiful eighth-grader."

"When did you find out?"

"The parade. That necklace he wears? She had one on just like it."

"Yeah, I found out about it, too . . . Well, maybe she'll dump him for some other guy, and then you let Jim cry on your shoulder and he'll realize he really likes you best."

I smiled. "You never give up, do you?"

"It could happen," she assured me. "Really. Anyway, you should go to the square dances on the pier. Jim goes, and you never know."

"I'd go if I had someone to dance with," I said. "Last year, when we were here visiting Aunt Jane, Mom was my partner, but now Mom has George."

"Well, I'd go with you if I were going to be here, but I'm not . . . Just think, Meg. No more spiders in the salad. No more green toothpaste."

"No more making a fool of myself in public."

"Yeah, you're going to really miss me."

I didn't say anything to that, but I thought missing

Micale would be like missing the pebble in my sneaker.

We got up and started walking back down the beach. "You know," Micale said, "I was sort of jealous of you because my mother thought you were so perfect. It made me mad that she wanted me to be like you."

"So? My mom told me to be more like you."

"You're kidding. Heather said that?"

"She thinks you're fun, Micale."

"But she thinks *you're* wonderful."

"Well, sure. I'm all she has."

"Yeah, if you think *that* didn't make me jealous," Micale said. "I mean, my mother treats me like I'm a mistake she got stuck with."

"She loves you. She just doesn't show it very well," I said confidently. "And you don't really act like you care about her . . . You and your mother need to work out how to get along."

"Maybe. Anyway, I meant to shake you up and I did."

"You sure did."

Ahead of us Billie was chasing a flock of herring gulls. They squawked furiously as they lifted their heavy wings and flew away. The fool dog came trotting back with a stone in her mouth and looked from one to the other of us hopefully.

"No stone throwing, Billie," Micale told her. "I'm too pooped."

I threw one stone and then another and another. It

was fun to see Billie galumphing over the sand after them. Fun to throw, too.

As soon as we got home I called Mom, who said she and George would take care of the crabs and not to worry and thanks. Then I drank a glass of milk and wondered how the house could be so quiet with Micale and Billie in it. When I looked for them, I found them sound asleep on Micale's bed. They looked cute, curled up there together.

Tomorrow Micale would be gone. Suddenly I was squeezed with regret. I *was* going to miss her. I really was. She was funny. Sometimes she was even lovable, and she did make my life exciting. I'd miss her. Yes, I would. The discovery was so surprising that it took me a few minutes before I began wondering what I could do about it.

What would Micale say if I asked her to stay? *Listen,* I could say, *it'll be too quiet here if you leave now.* But if Micale stayed, what then? She'd start pushing me to do something else I didn't want to do—like go to the square dances. She'd have me in a square with Jim and his girlfriend before I knew it, and then—then who knows what would happen? Maybe even something good.

I remembered the bubble pipe. Yeah, I thought, that's the way to tell her. I dug it out of my drawer while Billie watched, blinking her bumblebee yellow eyes at me. Bubbles. Bubbles lighter than air. I blew a whole flock of the rainbow-streaked balls at Billie who tilted her head this way and that as they floated over her. She looked so silly I giggled. Micale woke up.

"Am I dreaming?" she said. "Look at you, Meg, you're laughing and blowing bubbles just like a kid."

"Do you have to go tomorrow?" I asked her.

"Not really. The grandma is tough enough to deal with Ma without me."

"Good, then why don't you stay?"

"You want me to stay? The whole summer?"

"Yeah, I do."

"How come?"

I could see why she'd wonder after the mean things I'd said to her. I took a deep breath, and blew it out. "Because I like you a lot . . . Don't ask me why, though."

Her eyes widened. She grinned at me. "Know something, Meg? I like you, too. Isn't that weird when we're so different?"

"Weird," I said and blew a batch of bubbles her way. We both giggled at silly Billie, who crossed her eyes in amazement when one landed on her nose. "So what'll we do this afternoon?" I asked.

"Don't worry, I'll think of something," she said.

I groaned in mock despair, before I burst out laughing.